Hornytown Chutzpah

Hornytown Chutzpah

Andrew Hiller

Atthis Arts

Hornytown Chutzpah

Copyright © 2026 by Andrew Hiller

Cover Illustration and Design by Andrew Hiller

Edited by E.D.E. Bell

All rights reserved.

Published by Atthis Arts, LLC
Detroit, Michigan
atthisarts.com

ISBN 978-1-961654-38-9

Library of Congress Control Number: 2025950752

To my dad who taught me to value the serious and silly equally. Through him, I learned that every idea deserves honest scrutiny and an occasional nose tweak.

The Ten Commandments according to Sol the Wise Guy

I. *G_d's not the jealous type, but just like it goes with your mother, don't forget to call once in a while.*

II. *Don't fall for cons. Stay away from cults. Read the fucking fine print.*

III. *People love to misquote and manipulate scripture. That's a Pit trap, bubbelah.*

IV. *Work is good, but don't wear yourself down. Saturday's a good day to chill and maybe study your Torah a little bit.*

V. *Stop kvetching all the time. Love those who nurture and support you. Nurture and support them in return.*

VI. *Thou shalt not commit murder. No jokes on this one, kiddo.*

VII. *Keep your promises. Don't cheat. Don't allow your name and your word's value to fluctuate like a currency market.*

VIII. *Don't be a gonif.*

IX. *"Talk (bull)shit, get hit (by the bull)" or Don't bullshit unless you want to get the horns.*

X. *If you're not fucking two, don't take someone's toy just because they're playing with it.*

1.

The sheyd passed by my mezuzah like it was a smoke detector without a battery. The furshlugginer thing was supposed to protect the first born, but my dime store tchotchke just blinked blissful ambivalence. Underneath my desk, my toes clenched and unclenched.

"Never expected a personal escort," I said.

After giving my office the once-over, the sheyd directed her stony gaze my way. She had the kind of figure that would make a burlap sack look like a cocktail dress, a smile that suggested laser whitening, and eyes that seemed too damn articulate, like the judgment had already passed. Jews weren't supposed to believe in Hell, but after working the beat for a decade I knew the joint wasn't picky. At least she wasn't a dybbuk. Ghosts tend to cling and fill you with their bitterness.

Not that I believe in profiling.

"I need your help," she said.

Her voice had the husky charm of a chain smoker who had just spent the last five years in a walk-in humidor.

I stifled a laugh. Reached for the tumbler atop my file cabinet and downed a shot's worth of Manischewitz in one sweet gulp. For a moment, I lingered in the pleasure of sweet red. Then I caught sight of her again.

Damn.

Those legs. That face.

Don't do deals with the devil. That was the number one rule of police work. Mind you, I'm not a cop anymore, and she was only a demon.

Buying time, I tipped back my tumbler again, but with the exception of a few harmless red drops the vessel remained empty. I shook my head and realized I was coming in third in a race between arousal and panic.

"Sol?" she asked, draping her slightly pointed fingers over the back of the ladderback chair I use to interview clients.

My eyes drifted towards my bills even as the chair started to smoke. The 'overdue' stamps shone red. As I considered my answer, the demon tapped out her impatience. That beat restored my confidence. It was the sound of a client, not the rat-a-tat-tat of someone readying herself to take me out.

"I don't do Hornytown," I said, finally, with the kind of false bravado that made people call me dick instead of detective.

"That's not what I heard. Heard you used to haunt the place on the regular."

She leaned forward to show off her T-shirt. I stared at the big lollipop with its "Sucker for Sin" logo and swallowed.

It didn't matter that I knew she wasn't a she. Manly, femme, thick, thin, brown, white, tall, short, a succubus appears as whatever they think is most attractive to the person opposite them. It made them all but impossible for a mortal to ID.

I shuddered a long breath. All my immunity, all my built-up tolerance felt flushed.

She didn't laugh at my state of obvious discomfiture. That

surprised me, though it shouldn't have. Most of the seducers I'd met on the beat were very intuitive and damned good conversationalists. Not just about cards, but about botany, physics, psychology. After centuries dealing with sinners, those shedim knew all kinds of shit. Talking to them made me a better person. Sure, I started doing it for the leads, but shmoozing has a real way of erasing some preconceptions.

Truth is, most of the time, we just played cards. I brought wasabi peas and red hots. They furnished Oreos and M&M's. None of us drank. No one smoked. They used to joke that I better watch myself or I'd pawn my soul just to make ante.

Well, fuck.

Maybe I did owe Greenie and the girls a debt.

I decided to go formal. "What can I do for you, Miss . . . ?"

"Urrie," she said.

I winced. I hate puns.

"Ms. Urrie," I repeated and pulled out a standard dick contract.

The apple of her blood-colored cheek drew in like she was about to whistle. I waved off the tune. Last thing you want is to get sirened before you get the down payment. She started. The stutter sounded way too human. I waited. Gave her time to spill. Finally, she did.

"Sol, I've been framed for murder."

I did a doubletake. I had expected something bad. But murder? That, I didn't expect. In my head, my rabbi wagged his finger, "Boychik. Never face a demon without a good set of squishy orange earplugs and a full canister of Manischewitz. Better yet, a good bottle of Hayotzer Lyrica Mourvedre 2019."

I leaned back in my chair. Tented my fingers to prevent them from rubbing my temples.

Despite what everyone thinks, killing's not common in Hornytown. Sure, bribes flow fast and demons have been known to paint the town red with the blood of anyone who wants to pay off a bit of their debt before their eternal reckoning, but as the denizens say, Hell on Earth is a hell of a lot less scary than the Hell we made of Earth. In fact, Hornytown only ever rose up because the Devil took a trip to Mortalville about fifteen years ago.

You see, back then, during a vacation in Washington DC, the Sinner-in-Chief discovered that Hornytown's Tunnel of Love ride appeared quaint compared to everything free will inspired in the 'capital of the free world.' So, being practical, he relocated a branch office from the Pit and placed it in the 'burbs where his employees could upskill.

The result?

Not much.

Sure, there was a slight uptick in rush-hour congestion, but drugs, prostitution, robbery, assaults? All went down. And as far as demonic foul play goes, I never heard any chatter about AWOL demons breaking The Ten. From one point of view, I suppose that's not too surprising. After all, Hornytown sort of co-exists with the rest of Mortalville or the Earth as we humans call it, but still remains separate. To get there, you have to drive through one of DC's infernal traffic circles. Maybe that's why Urrie's statement spurred some deep-set fears about the day the demons stopped playing possum.

"Murder?" My nerves cha-cha-ed and I took three steps back before rocking forward towards my wine safe.

In her chair, Urrie remained as still as a trainer working with a skittish dog.

"Wet your whistle?" I asked. It was a see-through excuse to get to the soaker, but you work with what you got. For me, that meant a little kosher wine spiked with a kiddush. Others used different stock. I heard of one Catholic cop who kept a bag of sacramental wafers and threw 'em like blades. Wouldn't work for me, but different strokes, you know.

Hands kept behind her back, she offered me a little shrug. Cautiously, I turned my back on her, opened the safe door and found an empty canister. Beside it, six flacid water balloons hung and beneath them a red stain.

Fuck.

Now, every play was hers. I was out of time and ammo. Her head tilted, brow wrinkling just a little. I gawked at that face. She wore a perfect blend of Marilyn, Rita Moreno, and Halle Berry. It didn't matter that I knew it was an illusion. That that amalgamation was not her face. I leaned back, tried to work my way through the glamour to find her. There was something in the tilt of her head, the body language, something underneath the Marilyn mask she wore that made me bet she'd be hot no matter what form she chose.

Oy gevalt was I fucked.

With a shake of the head, she yanked a cup off the top of my stack of dollar store paper ones and strode towards the bookshelf. Her nose wrinkled in distaste as she surveyed my literature. Then, like she knew the place, she traced a finger over the spine of a book with a false cover. I stared, dry-throated, as she pulled a bottle of hooch I had forgotten about from its hiding place. With her teeth, she pulled the cork. She didn't bother to hide the fangs. After a perfect pour, she threw a measured shot in my face.

I sputtered.

Then, she refilled the cup and set it in front of me. "I can't help what I am, but I need you here. What's going on downstairs don't matter." Urrie leaned in. "So hard as it may be . . . I need you to be a detective and not a dick. I need Solomon the Wise Guy."

The name shocked me back as much as the sting of Scotch in my eyes. Solomon the Wise Guy was who I used to be. The guy who didn't play dirty. Who didn't drink. Who played everything straight. That was his rep, anyhow, even if sometimes Solomon Weiss looked the other way or got his hands greased while he tightroped the line between mensch and cop.

"Okay." I said and composed myself. "Tell me a story. Make it a good one."

Now, I been lied to plenty and I've been a sap more often than I'd like to admit, but the key to IDing a liar is that the truth always sounds preposterous. Lies? They come out clean and orderly. So I readied myself and hoped that my ears weren't as susceptible to her charms as the rest of me. "I didn't do it," she repeated, voice as scratchy as old vinyl.

"Get to the story. We've both worked with enough sinners to have heard that wash a million times."

Her shrug revealed a patch of skin to the right of her collarbone.

She walked around the desk towards me. My steps mirrored hers like we were playing a game of tag and keeping the desk between us was the only thing that could save me from becoming 'it'. Except, when she reached the safe base, she was the one who sat down. This, despite the fact that being wanted for murder definitely made her 'it'.

"I'm trying to tell you . . . I could never." She stopped there, a secret stuck in her craw.

Sand slid in the hourglass. Moments grew long. I broke first.

"Why?" I deadpanned, "Because you're such a good little shicksa?"

She turned towards the door, weighing whether to tell me something she wasn't sure she could. More seconds ticked away. I caught her scarlet stare in the reflection of the hat rack and her gaze flicked away the moment our eyes met in a way that suggested she felt conflicted. I didn't buy it. We both knew that by coming here, she'd already made her decision.

"No," she said haltingly, "I mean I can't."

"So," I said, pulling another gulp from the paper cup, "Why can't you?"

"I'm a demon." She sagged as if that explained everything. When she realized it didn't, she puffed out a little sigh. "Oh, I can torture, I can manipulate, I can even seduce and make a man wish for death, but I can't kill. It's outside the job description."

I waited her out. Like any vacuum, silence demands to get filled. With knuckles whitened, she gripped my hat rack so hard my fedora shook. Then, her head turned as she heard the warble of a fire truck, and she spilled.

"Once someone's killed," she leveled a look at me hotter than a mayonnaise facial at high noon in Death Valley, "the suffering's over. The job is torment. Eternal torment. So, we can't kill. Demons can't kill." She let me digest that. Taste the truth of it. Then spun away.

Well, fuck me. There it was. The simple truth. A truth so clean it sounded impossible.

Her claws extended, surprised that I got that out of her. What she just spilled was the kind of corporate secret that people paid a lot for. I mean, I couldn't even guess how much it was worth. Society's not about to get overrun. Demons have fucking lines.

A puzzle piece slid into place. This no-killing-meshuganah explained why she chose a dick instead of a lawyer. A lawyer would use this in her defense. A dick chases down clues. To earn my pay, I had to prove her innocent, not work an argument that gets her off the hook.

"Okay," I said, wanting a smoke for the first time in ten years, "who didn't you kill?"

The way her face brightened made my legs go weak. Again, she clasped her hands. The slap rang out like the sound of an angel getting its wings or a schlub like me getting a second chance.

"You believe me?" Surprise shocked the rasp out of her voice.

"I believe you," I affirmed, "but I might be the only one. People break company rules all the time. Just because it's against the company manual doesn't make the windmill grind. 'Thou shalt not kill' has never exactly stopped anyone before."

Her hair fell below her eyes.

She glanced at the radio resting on my file cabinet, noticed the dangling electrical cord.

"You haven't guessed?" she said. "I thought everyone'd be talking about it by now."

I pushed back from the desk. The warble grew louder and it wasn't a single bird, but a whole flock. I tweaked open the blinds to catch a glimpse of lit billboards and a line of blue and white ants flashing their way to my doorstep. Urrie studied me over my shoulder. This was my last chance to do the right thing. This was my last chance to do the good thing. Wish I knew which was which.

Wee-owww! blared the sirens.

"How big is this, Urrie?"

"We have to go. If you're going to help me, we have to go now."

Outside, the sirens roared close enough that I expected to hear feet pounding on the stairs any second. I checked Urrie out. It surprised me how much seeing a scared demon hit me. I finished off the Scotch.

2.

Pulled by the call and response of the sirens, I pressed my hands against the windowpane. Oscillating red climbed up the alleyway until it spilled over into my office. I counted Ford Interceptors. Someone had called in the whole force. Urrie approached the window but I waved her back, needing some plausible deniability. I watched as the blue boys stormed the building.

"No time to run," I said.

Surveying our options, I found few.

My office is spare: a desk, two bookshelves, a wine safe, and a dented-up file cabinet.

"Bathroom," I suggested. "Pull the shower curtain."

Urrie's nose wrinkled as I slammed the door after her. Guilt crept up my spleen. That there was something bad enough in there to offend a demon's olfactory system worried me. Mother would have yoikered that her reaction proved how far I had let myself go. I set the emotion aside as a problem for another day.

With care, I draped a tie over the knob in the faint hope that it would look like a coat closet. Then, I spritzed the office generously with sanitizer. Finally, for the sake of the front door, I turned the lock and swung it wide open. There was no pretending I hadn't heard the cops. No point in absorbing the property damage if they decided to barge their way in.

Bang. Bang. Bang.

I stuck my mug out of the office to find the bookkeepers, ambulance chasers, and the fortune teller who sidelined as a massage therapist closing shop for the day. Lucky for them, I took the office opposite the stairwell. Paid a little extra for it because I like to have a way out. Soon enough, I heard feet pounding up the stairs. I leaned against the door jamb, folded my arms across my chest and waited.

"Evening, boys," I said to the first blue boy who emerged from the stairwell.

He stopped dead, face flushed, belly bellowing from the exertion. Three flights at a dead sprint can take a lot out of a desk jockey. The beat cops behind him took it slower. I pictured them a floor down with hands itching to draw and eyes on the hunt for signs of bad intention.

The desk jockey and I engaged in a staring contest until Alfreda Connors elbowed past him. The lieutenant's jacket hung tight across her shoulders, suggesting body armor. Only thing on her not by the book was a heart-shaped locket that looked old enough to be a family heirloom.

She flashed a badge at me like we didn't know each other, like she hadn't been my boss for six years. I waved hello and asked if she minded wiping her feet before she entered. By that time, six of her bully boys had arrived.

"Lieutenant," I said.

I noticed that she smartly let the desk jockey cross the threshold to my office doorway first just in case there was hellfire awaiting the first sucker to trip a ward line. By then, the beat cops had caught up. They were big boys with shaggy mustaches.

"Mind wiping your feet before you enter," I said to them. "Just had the place cleaned."

That brought them up short. Their mouths sagged with the disappointment of not needing to break my door down. Myself, my shoulder never liked that kind of thing.

"Solomon the Wise Guy," one of the bullies growled. "Always knew you would get mixed up with some bad cookies."

I didn't recognize the badge. Pimpled punk probably rose after I left the force. Like I said, he was big. Looked like the kind of shmuck who joined the force because it gave him permission to beat people up.

"Officer," I answered, ignoring the intimidation shtick. "Can I help you?"

Conners, with an aggrieved look on her punim that said I had put her through this one too many times, took charge.

"Out of our way, Sol. We got a report a bad demon was holing up with you."

I chuckled.

"Bad demon. Ain't that a bit redundant, Lieutenant?"

Her expression indicated a lack of appreciation for my observation. With a weariness well earned, she jabbed a finger at me so hard it made the heart-shaped locket leap off her Kevlar. I rubbed my chest. It didn't actually hurt. Really, it failed to do anything more than draw my eyes to the fact that she lacked papers in either hand.

For what it's worth, I wasn't going to demand a warrant. Didn't want Connors to think I had anything to hide or that I wanted to play it difficult. Besides, she would get in now or fifteen minutes from now, and if I made her wait, her bully boys would be upset I made them miss their dumbbell time. I wanted these cowbells feeling lazy. At the very least, I didn't need them breaking my stuff.

"Come on in. There's some coffee left in the pot. Tastes like drek, but feel free to grab a cup."

Connors barged past like it was a win. Set her badges to work. They turned over my desk, flung my chair, tipped over my file cabinet, upended my bookshelves.

They found nothing.

Connors' ear twitched.

"Where is she?"

"I sent her packing," I said with a shrug. "She headed south. Uptown."

The nerve. Connors didn't believe me. She ordered her boys to give the place another once over. By then, another six had joined the party. I gave her a 'you break it you bought it' stare, but we both knew I didn't have the coin to get a lawyer to make good on the threat.

The blue boys looked under the rug as if Urrie could flatten herself to a piece of cardboard. I laughed, but maybe she could. With grubby hands they tilted lampshades, slid the desk drawers open. Pried open my wine safe so violently, I feared I'd need to borrow a sledgehammer to bang it closed. Inside, the sight of my deflated water balloons felt like an indictment. They were so far gone that the wine had dissolved the rubber and left a stain on the shelf.

While they worked, I allowed my eyes to rove. One of the first things you learn is that cops look where you're looking and where you're not looking. So, if you want to give them nothing, look everywhere. It wasn't hard. The blue shirts were messing up my shit.

"Connors," I said with a hint of annoyance, "tell them to clean up after."

"Bill the department," she answered, but motioned for them to slow down. After the third blue shirt passed the bathroom without opening the door, I wondered if Urrie had projected a glamour to hide herself. More likely, their lizard brains smelled something that urged them to stay away. Most people, even good ones, feel a little reluctant to go face to face with a demon and chances are these cops weren't that aspirational breed of cop.

Searching their faces, I doubted they practiced enough self-reflection to realize it.

"So, Connors, seriously. What's with all this mishigas? What she do? How big a score I blow this time?"

With a leveling gaze, Connors waved her men outside the office.

"Pretty big one," she admitted. "Demon we're looking for went rogue. Killed the mayor of Hornytown."

I took a step back. My shoulders hit the wall.

"Jesus," I said, pulling in help from wherever. "Your reports must have got it wrong. Even the big reds don't mess with the Unicorn."

Connors crossed herself, then helped me flip my desk upright. Kneeling, she shuffled through a few papers looking for red ink. A blood contract. I had none. None in the desk anyway.

"It's the real thing, Sol. We got civilians fleeing Hornytown without going through any of the checkpoints. Whole place is in a panic. Nobody seen anything like this since the damned place rose up."

I exhaled.

"Yeah," she agreed.

"And you really think I'd get mixed up in something like that?"

She took a beat then went there.

"You're the only cop I know who likes Hornytown. Only one I know who reupped his beat there twice."

"Things change."

She smacked her lips. "So you say."

"I'm not a cop anymore, Connors."

"Look," she said. "Word is you're a friend. Someone on the run is looking for a friend."

I considered laying down some schmutz about Hornytown, but the more you talk the more you're likely to trip yourself up, and Connors wasn't a fool. Still, I couldn't help trying to point the finger just a little.

"I could point you in the direction of some blue boys who enjoy their downtime there."

"Only for the perks, Sol. Only for the perks. You're the only one who ever bought a ring."

Well, fuck.

3.

Ronald (the Unicorn) Hart moved into Hornytown with the goal of carving his name into every circle. With blueprints in hand from never-paid architects, he took up residence in an abandoned castle on the border of Bethesda and Hell. From the beginning, Hart went big, hiring artists who specialized in Gothic art, dystopian cover art, and B-movie horror posters. Within months, the most cliché barbed, spiked, gargoyled building ever made vomited forth. It was the kind of horror that demons and critics averted their eyes from, but that fit the tourist-*fairytale* version of Hell perfectly.

Hart's pitch *Remove the threat of eternal torment at the cost of a three-day-all-expenses-paid-vacation* proved popular. Didn't hurt that the deal came complete with an endless buffet and spa treatments either. And the souvenirs? You wouldn't believe how much people pay to own a genuine piece of Hell, but as the wise say, *Always read the fine print, bubbeleh.*

~

Connor's fixed her eyes on mine. "If a demon even steps out of Hornytown, that's an all call. I don't care if it's one of the Unicorn's boogeymen or a regular red. You're on notice, Weiss.

You harbored a demon. I've got three birdies who say you knew one crossed the border."

I lowered my eyes and made the appropriate mutterings. Not once during her dressing down did I glance at the bathroom. Unsatisfied and perhaps looking for a fight, she kept going, telling me "I knew better" and that I had to "pick the right side!"

When finally the door closed behind her, I counted the ways I had just fucked up my life. After number twenty-seven, my lamp started to flicker because, of course, a bulb would choose today to go out, unless it was the utilities proclaiming they were done with me paying a few bucks under the minimum every month.

Over the dark glass, I muttered a blessing for the candles. It sparked, then glowed. Might have been the words. Might have been me screwing the bulb tighter into the socket. All I know is I'm not sure I could have handled it if the light vanished on the day Hornytown came back into my life.

Shortly after my prayer, Urrie staggered out of the bathroom and collapsed onto my desk. She bore all the symptoms of major mojo expenditure. She looked like a nifla: red cheeks faded to sallow yellow, flaking scales . . . the whole bit. With care, I grabbed my overcoat and threw it over her. Then, like a well-trained boy, I dashed to my lunch bag and pulled out a ham and cheese. The two pieces of bread were fit for brick duty and the mayo smelled a bit off, but I gave it to her anyway. She inspected the offering balefully.

"Demons don't do spoiled," she moaned. "We punish the spoiled."

I studied my mess to see what else I had. Being raised by a Jewish mother, I had to offer food, and somewhere in this office a stashed bag of red hots hid.

"I'll be fine." She waved off the search. "Just overextended myself."

I massaged my jaw while trying to work out what to do about the demon wanted for murder splayed on my desk. No good ideas came to mind. After a bit, she conceded, "My powers are more finite outside of Hornytown. I just need . . ." a look of embarrassment crossed her face, "I just need one."

"Need one what?" I said. I mean I knew she was a succubus, but this wasn't really the time or place.

"A little one will do," she pleaded.

"Just a quickie?"

She sneered in repulsion. "No." Then, in a voice pitched to cow unruly children, she explained, "I burn sins when I . . ." Her fingers fluttered. "I need to eat a sin. It doesn't have to be a big one."

Oh.

It wasn't a small ask. A sin given to a demon can never be redeemed. It's a permanent marker against your soul. Add up enough of those and things get toasty. My chest tightened at the thought. Little chance as I had to escape my fate, I didn't want to give a sin away for nothing.

"Saving me might be worth a counterbalance," she bartered.

I prepared to refuse, but watching the tremble of her breath, I bent. How a guy with a hero complex could ever say no to a succubus is something I'd argue at the time of

Judgment, even if it's a defense that would get me laughed out of court.

"Back when I was a kid," I told Urrie, "maybe eight or nine, I stole my mother's gun. It was a .22, but the meanest thing I ever saw. The thing was so black it swallowed light. Heavy, too. I had to hold it two-handed to aim it."

Urrie perked up. I had her attention.

She cupped her hand under her chin, some cock's comb rose already seeping into the canary tone of her skin. She looked better, and I hadn't even got to the sin part unless 'thou shalt not steal' was enough to satisfy her. I guess I should have stopped right there, but her gaze sucked the rest of the story out of me.

"Sometimes a boy wants to impress his friends. Show off, you know?"

A nod. Such a friendly nod. Like that of a psychologist or a priest taking confession. 'Tell me my son. Let us share this burden.'

"We met at Sligo Creek, my friends and me, just a little down the bike trail and pushed into the woods. My palms were all sweaty. Akhmed put lookouts out to make sure no one could see us. Then on some stumps, we set up the beer cans."

"You were drinking at eight?" The husk was back in her voice.

"No," I waved her off. "We found those in a trashcan outside a 7-Eleven."

She nodded, disappointed.

"I fired off the first round. Missed from five feet. Probably was more the nerves than the kick. Hornytown hadn't emerged yet, but I knew what I was doing was wrong. Exciting, but wrong."

An encouraging nod drew me forward.

"The beer cans mocked me. None even wobbled. Joe and Amallah took their turns. Showed me how it was done. They called me names. All the good I'd done my rep by bringing the gun was getting washed away because I was such a bad shot. I started yelling and telling them that this wasn't fun. That I'd do better if it were real. They egged me on. Dared me to prove myself. Only did it because they wanted more time with the gun. I gave in to save my rep.

"I set up a shot that was a good twenty feet away. Mimicking some TV big shot I kept the gun at my hip so I could quick draw. Shoot without even aiming.

"Pop, pop, pop. I pulled off three shots.

"Something screeched. In a panic, I fired three more rounds. Still never hit a can, but I got the bird."

The tears in my eyes surprised me.

"First life I ever took. Only life I ever took."

To my surprise, Urrie offered me a sympathetic tilt of the head. A glow suffused her. Her complexion shone with a kind of after-dinner contentment. I don't know how demons count sin, but from her expression she liked hers well-aged.

"Never played with a gun after that," I finished up. "That was all it took for me to realize what guns were for."

She thanked me.

I grunted, turned back to the matter at hand.

"Urrie," I began before exploding, "what the Hell? You killed the fucking Unicorn?"

She glared at me. Madder at my accusation than about slandering her home.

"I told you I didn't do it."

"The fucking unicorn?"

"Listen to me."

"Ronald fucking Hart?"

She slapped me. The heat from her palm scalded my cheek. The pain startled me. Shut me up.

"It's not like I didn't want him gone," she said. "We all did."

My yap itched to open, but I shook the instinct.

Collect statements, I told myself. Gather evidence. Ask more questions.

"Did you have access to him? Did he know you?"

Urrie looked away.

"Oh Urrie," I said.

"Yeah, I know. Motive and opportunity, but it's not like I'm the only one."

"Then why . . . Why did the entire force just come to my door looking for you?"

When she settled her hand on my desk, the wood sizzled. Embarrassment widened her eyes. I didn't buy it. I knew that if the bully boys came back and saw it, it was a 'Go to jail/Don't collect $200' moment.

"I had access to the penthouse suites," she continued on like she hadn't just marked me. "Carried the cash sometimes. Hart liked us to dump the bills on his bed and he'd jump onto them like he was Scrooge McDuck." Something in my expression made her feel the need to explain how she'd fallen into an errand girl role. "Ronald has a way of making everyone slip down a peg. Working for him, I earned chits, markers that needed erasing. But it wasn't me that offed him. I'm just the one who found pieces of him."

She saw the disbelief.

"Sol. You don't know what it's like at Hart's Keep. Demons punishing demons . . . Sinners living out their cruelest dreams. Plus, Hart never pays anyone. He screws everyone he goes into business with. It could have been anyone. Anyone."

She slumped into my ladderback chair with enough self-control not to burn it, reached for the bottle of hot sauce I kept on the corner of my desk and guzzled it down like it was a coke.

I tapped my chin. Considered my next step.

My hesitation had nothing to do with guilt. I've taken plenty of jobs where I didn't believe the client because there's this thing called rent. But shooting a few dirty pictures or dumpster diving to find some shit to use against a gonif landlord was different than this. The trembles from this earthquake would reverberate. This case mattered.

"One more question," I said, riffling through boilerplate pages the blue boys had dumped on the floor. She stared, waited. "Why me? Why not just burrow down to a circle where no one could touch you?"

She didn't answer immediately. Maybe she had no answer. The wait started taking on a familiar gravitational pull. This time, I broke first.

"I need to know, Urrie," I blurted. "Why me?"

She pouted her lips. Batted those long lashes. I counted

to ten before I looked back. She was scratching trails into the armrests, leaving more evidence. Evidence the blue boys would know wasn't there when they had searched the place.

"Sol," she said, "I don't know who I can trust. Justice has become a lonely orphan. The Unicorn's goons have been arranging damnation for guys with clean ledgers . . . and no one's doing . . . and, well, everyone knows when a Hornytown girl gets in trouble she can count on the Wise Guy." When she saw me unmoved, she pulled out the big guns. "Sol, don't you believe in tikun olam anymore? Your duty to repair the world? Please, please help me, Sol."

She ended with the dirtiest line of all.

"You're my only hope."

4.

With a hoodie over her head and a bulky coat draped across her shoulders, Urrie took the stairs two at a time. Our goal was my thirty-year-old avocado-colored Toyota Echo. The ecobox fit me well, but with those legs, she'd probably feel as compressed as an NBA center flying economy.

We dodged celebrity twice by turning our heads just before the glint of a lens appeared. As the building's resident dick, I got hired to set up the security system so I knew where all the cameras were. Urrie followed cues as if wired into my head. Four floors down, we reached the level marked PG 1. The last camera jumped out at us like a paparazzi sniffing out a sunbathing royal, but with a timely tug at my fedora it likely only got my chin. Urrie ignored it and pointed at the box by the door.

I smirked. The thing was purely for show. Our building's card reader hasn't worked for about three years. Fearing no security ping, I pushed the door open and gallantly waved her through.

Gunshots rang out.

I dove to the side. The door cooperatively slammed behind me. Plinks of something low caliber struck the metal door and failed to make their way through. Urrie stood in front of the framework as if unused to the concept of pain or mortal harm. I wondered if she'd even ever gotten a faceful of Manischewitz.

Despite my best attempt to motion her back, the

meshuginah sheyd swung the door open and stormed into battle. A moment later, I heard more pops, followed by the thump of a head striking a hood. Before I could decide whether I had her back, tires screeched. I ducked even though I was the one behind a metal door. A moment later, I heard a crunch. A big one. Carefully, I edged the door open.

Across from a parking lot support column lay the totaled rear end of an SUV. I whistled, imagining Urrie hulking out and tossing cars like cardboard boxes.

Recognizing that few bad guys aim for the feet, I dropped to my knees and reached for my mother's old sidearm, but my hands only found the rubber of wine-filled balloons. I shook my head. I had planned for Hornytown. What good is a gun in Hell?

I considered running upstairs, but to my surprise, no spray of bullets flew overhead. Instead, I found Urrie holding up a pinstriped tough guy by his collar. His wingtips dangled. The guy looked so freaked out he didn't even try to kick away.

In the garage, Urrie changed hats. No longer was she the sexy succubus, but a scaled and horned monster that probably moonlit as a Pit torturer. I swallowed as her knife-blade wings flared. Made a note to play nice. Her admission that she didn't kill wasn't enough to lower my heartrate. After all, the difference between seduction and pain can be pretty thin.

"Confess your sins to me," she ordered Pinstripes.

Her voice filled the garage.

"Errrgh," Pinstripes said.

I counted six holes in Urrie's hoodie. A burn mark on her cheek suggested at least one bullet struck home, but none of that fazed her. With a snkkkt, she loosed five claws that shone like switchblades. My attraction to her failed to shrivel up as much as it should have.

"Jurisdiction," I said, stepping up to her and giving her an excuse not to kill. She turned towards me and her head morphed from something angular and jagged to something more '80s supermodel. She winked at me.

Good to know she remained in control. I wasn't sure I was.

"Jurisdiction," I repeated.

She shook Pinstripes like it was taking everything she had not to overstep.

"Don't give this drek an out," I bullshitted, implying that even Hell suffered from shysters who worked loopholes.

She lifted the goon higher, still only holding onto the fabric of Pinstripes' jacket. A close inspection revealed that none of the wool smoked. I smiled. She hadn't Hulked out. She had Batmanned.

"Be good," she warned Pinstripes. Her voice throbbed throughout the garage like a jacked-up bass.

The goon nodded, whiter than a full moon covered in fresh snow.

I walked up to Pinstripes and slapped him gently on the cheek. His eyes never flicked my way. He only had eyes for Urrie. I didn't blame him. A trickle of shame slithered up my neck. Bubbe had never raised me to like bad girls.

"Boychik," I said forcefully. He didn't turn his head, but I knew he heard me. "Boychik," I repeated and stepped closer. "Repent and study your Torah."

Something hate-filled clicked then. I noted the king of hearts tattooed onto his neck fielded a swastika in its crest at the same time I registered the .38 still in his hand. I recoiled, knowing this would be the third time a bullet would enter my body. I'd been lucky to survive the first two. I didn't really want to face the charm.

Of course Urrie hadn't bothered to disarm him; she had no reason to fear a slug.

As Pinstripes raised the piece towards my head, a sharp-toothed grin stretched his face. The gun looked like a semi-automatic, but I know my super soakers better than I do mortal arms and at this range it didn't matter. One shot would do. But before he fired, Urrie tossed Pinstripes straight up.

The gun flared. A shot sped past me somewhere off to the right. I heard a sickening thud. Pinstripes let out an "eep!" as his head struck the ceiling of the parking garage, then he crumpled to the ground. I booted the gun out of his hand before checking his pulse. Well, fuck me, the lucky bastard was still kicking.

I glanced at Urrie, wondering if she had told the truth. Maybe she really couldn't kill. Maybe she could jam a man into a set of helicopter blades and he'd walk away with a clean shave.

Better sense told me not to dwell, so I patted his pockets, found his wallet and ripped all his business cards out. To inconvenience him, I took his driver's license, too. Bastard deserved a long wait at the DMV for trying to take a shot at me. "Take a number, buddy," I murmured as I gave the card a look.

A quick glance at his name confirmed I'd never heard of him. I stifled a sigh, then felt a comforting hand rest on my shoulder. I shrugged Urrie off. Not now, my gesture said. I wasn't sure when I'd be able to chase down who these rats were, but at least I had an ID and a list of associates.

"We should hit the road," I said, giving the guy a last look.

Before leaving, I snapped off a few shots on my phone of his tats. On the other side of the swastika, Pinstripes had stamped some kind of vampire stag. I ran both images against my mental rolodex of druidic and undead cults but drew a blank. For a moment, I wondered if Pinstripes really had been after Urrie, but the face he made when he saw me argued otherwise.

Besides, if he were going demon hunting why bring a pea shooter to a soaker fight? Better question, why not tote some chicken soup? Sure, Hornytown and the Feds signed some treaties against the stuff because Bubbe's chicken soup was just too potent, but since when did that matter to the bad guys?

A toe nudged me, turning my attention away from the crime scene. I was really tempted to check out the goons in the SUV, but Urrie's left foot was right. I rose, dusted my slacks, and started walking.

"Which one's yours?" Urrie's face held no emotion. Tossing a car, being shot at, concussing a would-be killer— None of this left a mark on her. That scared me a bit. More than her manhandling the punk, if I'm going to be honest.

"Thirty-year old green Echo," I said. "The one in need of a paint job."

She located it and frowned. My car's hardly a showpiece. The peeling paint looks like flaking skin after a sunburn and the dings, bumps, and scratches do nothing to sexy the shmata up. On the plus side, the rust spot patterns apparently appealed to her because after seeing them she reverently mouthed the word "circles".

With a turn of a key, I unlocked my ride. Being short, I fit the ecobox just fine. Like I expected, Urrie glanced up and down her six foot five form and shook her head. Before I had a chance to suggest she make like Bumblebee and transform, she sloughed off a gob of red goo.

The transmutation wasn't movielike. There was no snapping of limbs or arching of the back. No frame-by-frame distortion. Only a kind of putty-like remodeling as if she were being resculpted. Afterwards, she slid five foot four into the passenger seat. Being a gentleman, I chose not to comment. Instead, I whistled and turned the ignition.

5.

There's been much debate over why the Devil chose DC when he decided to raise up a corner of hell into Mortalville fifteen years ago. Hornytown isn't Biblical Hell. Mostly, it's for hands-on lessons so demons could interface with humans to learn what bad really looks like and for some tourists who want to play devil but don't want to take the heat of the actual Pit. Some blame Hornytown's emergence on recent politics. Me? I think it goes all the way back to George Washington.

You see, in 1791 after the decision was made to move the capital from New York to the Potomac, Washington recruited a Frenchman by the name of Pierre Charles L'Enfant. The gig he offered was to design a city worthy of the new American democracy.

"But," the General warned, the job had a catch.

"Sir," Washington reportedly told L'Enfant, "we know the British will return and we do not have the army to stop them. Would you design our district such that the Red Coats get delayed on their march to the capital? Even better, engineer it so the entirety of the British invasion finds themselves lost. Can you do this, sir? Are you up to the task?"

Up to the challenge, L'Enfant designed a city incorporating such a maze of circles that to this day tourists and locals find themselves spun around. I can't tell you how many times friends have wound up in Southeast when their goal was the

White House. Even GPS seems at a loss to solve the mystery of DC's streets.

Now, some reject this story. They claim the circles were not an attempt by L'Enfant to confound the British, but rather were put in as an homage to his hometown of Paris. Others speculated that the dirty dealings and use of enslaved labor in DC's creation created a kind of sympathetic resonance. Whichever it was, when the Devil went shopping for real estate, he found that the circles of Hell and the circles of DC fit like a glove. And so, with a total disregard to planning permits and payoffs, Hornytown was thrust upwards.

6.

The green Toyota Echo wove in and out of traffic like a pinball barely clever enough to avoid the bumpers. All the way down Connecticut Blvd., electric eyes crouched behind bushes at the bottom of the steepest downhill inclines. A speed trap hell for commuters on the way to actual Hell.

Urrie's head twisted all the way back as we passed Einstein's Bagels. After her mojo workout, I suppose she wanted some good carbs and a schmear. Guilt almost made me swing around, but I didn't risk it. Her scarlet skin stood out too much and the last thing we needed was a pit stop turning into a *Pit* stop. She huffed as we cruised on in the middle lane at a comfortable five miles an hour over the speed limit. Soon enough, the shop faded from sight.

I entered the circle at the intersection of Connecticut and Eastern Avenue which served as one of the borders between Hornytown and Mortalville as well as Chevy Chase and Washington, and flipped over the blindfold to cover my rearview mirror. Dante and Virgil didn't get much right, but I took no chances when it came to the danger of looking back. As we crossed the border, hellfire sizzled over the car's roof. Like revenge, Hornytown's flames ran cool. Each lick married the guilt carried on your shoulders to whatever you're most afraid of. To avoid the worst of it, I covered my eyes, but I was too slow.

Right there in front of my closed eyes, my mother materialized.

~

I'm eleven and standing to the side of a Bimah with a bunch of other kids in the chorus. My mother waves at me. Gives me a thumbs up. We both know I don't know how to read a character of Hebrew. To get around that, for about a month, mom and the cantor drill songs into me. By the time of my solo, I know all the sounds, but nothing about what those phonemes mean. I flex my fists and tell myself tonight isn't a big deal. I don't believe me, but I'm here, so I fill my belly up with air and prepare to belt out the first note.

My moment arrives and I panic. Searching for help, my eyes fall onto the music sheets, but the safety net of those alien characters mean nothing to me. Not even the cantor's prompting helps.

Eventually, with an arm over my shoulders, I was led away from God by the rabbi.

~

We breached Hell. Dante once wrote that the first circle of Hell was the domain of the virtuous unbaptized, so maybe that's why hellfire brings me back onto the Bimah three times out of ten. The rabbi I see twice a year on the High Holidays would say it's a message that it's not too late.

I blinked in an attempt to clear my head. Rating my screwups, this one really wasn't so bad except for that it cemented the realization that I was never going to get any Bar Mitzvah loot. To this day, that part hurts.

I forced the past out of my eyes as Urrie yanked the steering wheel, causing the car to jerk to the right. A gargoyle-laden edifice of black and crimson careened towards us. Like everything else here in Hornytown, this landscape had been personalized. My brain tended towards lakes of fire and creepy castles because my understanding of hell had been cobbled together from old sitcoms, comic books, and movies.

At my approach, the edifice lowered one of its towers like a knight readying its lance. I slammed the brakes with both feet.

By my side, Urrie, a bit more prudent, reached into my cup holder and dug around for some change. There wasn't much there. Just the stuff I kept there for parking meters.

"Quarters?" Her derision was real. "Where are your half dollars? Don't you have a Kennedy half dollar?"

Fuck, I thought, remembering I needed two silver coins to pay the toll. As a cop, I never had to pay. For a moment, I considered pulling out my credit card, but who could afford Hell's interest rates?

Besides, the lake is death, not damnation. Death is strictly *Pay on Delivery*.

"Will a filling do?" I asked.

I regretted making the offer when Urrie's nails sharpened into claws.

"Kidding. Oy vey! I was Kidding. Put those things away."

We were interrupted by an eel-like toll taker with a lion's mane. It gave us the once over and purred, "If you don't have silver or a pass, the river will take your sin."

"Get lost," I swerved in a vain attempt to shake the snake, but instead of losing the eel-thing, it struck the bumper and flopped onto the roof.

My instinct cried out, 'if one thing doesn't work try the other thing,' so I slammed my foot against the gas pedal even though I know pumping fossil fuels is a better way to speed your way into hell than to lose a demon. I glanced towards Urrie, hoping for a helpful suggestion, but she'd gone all crimson. You'd think this kind of effort would be required to get out of Hornytown . . . Not in.

"I gave at the office," I screamed out the window. Which wasn't just a line. If you remember, I just gave up a sin to Urrie an hour ago.

Dissatisfied with my lack of cooperation, the eel-thing wrapped itself around the Echo and plunged its front end into the soup of hellfire. Green smoke coagulated around us. I flicked my window wipers to try to clear away the memories the lake hungered to stuff into my lungs. Beside me, unhelpfully, Urrie started to roll down the windows. Probably figured the car was toast and we'd have to swim for it. I flinched as she undid my lap belt.

When the Echo resurfaced, I saw the fins of white picket fence posts, like something formed out of the hell of 1940's domesticity, cutting towards us. Now, I may not be Jewish enough to earn my Bar Mitzvah, but I knew enough to recognize that the eel-thing and the fence posts weren't inviting me to a land of milk and honey. In desperation, I reached under my shirt and ripped my Chai off. The necklace broke with a tink.

"You can't offer that," Urrie cried.

"It's silver," I rebutted.

Hellfire bellowed over us like wild surf. Between each flame lick, bulbs of gelatin salad surfaced. Inside the dessert, green seedless grapes, red veined with hungover irises stared at me like I was the only Waffle House left after a bender. I screamed.

Straining to throw my Chai. Urrie clutched my wrist.

"Let me go," I told her.

Something beneath us punctured. I took a peek outside the half-open window to discover a swarm of fuzzy bunny slippers termiting my tires.

What is this hell? It is mine.

"I need you," Urrie said. "Don't throw your life away."

She pried my hand open and the Chai fell somewhere in the crack between the car seat and the door. I shrieked. It had fallen into a worse place than a single sock in a dryer.

Out of silver, out of time, and out of luck, Hornytown was treating me like a kid trying to sneak into Disneyland.

"I can't help you if they get me," I said and something in my face must have registered enough fear that Urrie did something I'd never seen a demon do.

She gave up one of her own sins.

She gave one up for me.

"I loved," she said.

The lake burped, satisfaction flavoring its gas.

For a moment, I felt confusion, then the eel-thing hurled the Echo into the air. My beloved econobox bounced six times against the rubbled shoreline of Hornytown before landing in a tangle of licorice-colored XLR cables. I crawled out of the car and dizzily tracked the source to a window with cracked white paint. From that orifice, hundreds of mic cables slopped out like spaghetti down a pink-slimed brick wall mortared with ear wax.

Back here, really back, nostalgia crept like phlegm up my throat. To my surprise, I missed the joint.

Stooping, I petted the landlines that carried the vibration of confessions towards judgment. They purred their secrets at my touch. Back during my beat days, I had collected a lot of evidence this way. Further on, the XLR's split, connecting everything from podium microphones to the instruments of musicians condemned to never play anything other than their greatest hit.

As if on cue, an electric guitar did its best chalkboard scratch. I nodded towards Mozart. Dude played the hell out of his ax. Part of me wanted to thrash, but my head spun too much to bang. I turned in a circle, pretending to get my bearings, but really just soaking it all in.

From a nearby window, an AR-15 rattled off school lessons to white supremacists, shooting them whenever they got the syntax wrong. A pig sty mucked with factory runoff served as a dining table for CEOs.

I missed a step. Faltered. Recalled that the gravity of Hornytown was ten percent stronger than on Earth, but only on the right side of the body. The pull dragged my lips downward, giving me the permanent smirk I'll wear during my time here. As the reality of my return continued to hit me, Urrie grabbed my sleeve.

"We have to scram," she told me.

I knew a place near here where we could lay low but let her lead me anyway. Where she took me might tell me something. Might hold a clue.

If I was lucky, it would also hold some booze and a medic.

7.

Poker chips lined the streets like rusty fallen leaves. There's cash, too. The rubles, yuan, dollars, and euros all bore the faces of missing souls. The scatter's everywhere, but only the greenest tourist grabbed for any. I knelt down to examine a batch, but bounty hunters, eager to exchange their debt with another's, elbowed me aside.

Pro tip: Earthly coin rarely results in heavenly reward. Not that I judge. We all gamble. When boiled down, what else is free choice?

Urrie led me into a brothel that exited through the vent shaft of a laundromat. I followed on my hands and knees, a penitent. The path she chose did little to ease the bumps and bruises I got from the Echo's rough landing.

A grate creak later, a pair of fuzzy hands pulled me onto a disco-styled dance floor. Around the walls, the neon couches, glitter ball, and flashing squares shifted fast enough to make a body seize, but just before I passed out, I was guided to a backstage dressing room and plopped onto a furry Laz-E-Boy recliner whereupon Urrie announced, "I got him. You said I couldn't, but I got him to come back."

I blinked. Saw lights with my eyes open and with them closed. A green puppet with an inflatable face approached. Brusquely, they pushed a bowl of M&Ms at me and I shoveled a handful into my mouth. The sugar helped me orient.

Urrie went for a second candy dish, but the puppet slapped her hands away.

"Dicks prefer nuts," they said. My smirk grew more lopsided and I chuckled at one of my old lines being thrown in my face.

"Urrie," I explained to Greenie, one of my ex-cardplaying pals, "was never part of our games."

The puppet raised their control rod, combed their fingers through their hair. The coolness of the gesture made me shiver.

Back during my days on the beat, Greenie taught me to look past the caricature and understand that demons could be people. They showed me a lot of things like how to look beyond the hand to see the game really being played. Yeah, with Greenie, every move had a purpose. Take their face, early on, they'd shift around, trying out different forms just to get a reaction out of me. This one first manifested during a gin rummy game. I remember looking up and boom, there was this puppet.

"I told her not to bring you here," Greenie said.

I stared at them in all their puppety glory. Don't ask me why they look that way. I'm not in charge of what I find sexy.

Not really.

"This is a mortal crime," Urrie argued. "We need someone with expertise in mortal crimes."

Greenie flicked a felt hand in my direction. "Sol left the table and never made good. Lacks the chits to buy his way back in."

I raised a finger. Dropped it. Pounded the arm rest. In the

background of my memory, I heard the riffle of cards. Stopped myself from making excuses.

"Ms. Urrie dealt me in," I said, "then someone shot at me. Maybe it's not your call whether I'm in." There. Take that.

I chomped more M&Ms. Requested something to wet my whistle.

Confronted by one of their own rules, *You can't stop a game once it's started*, Greenie smiled. To get the ball rolling again, I ticked off some facts. "Here's what I know: Urrie's scared, on the lam, and accused of . . ."

Every hand in the room rushed to cover my mouth.

"Sweetie, we don't say the M word in vain."

After I nodded understanding, Greenie released their grip on my yapper and Urrie demanded an apology. Accused me of almost treading on The Sixth. But Greenie stuck to business. Said, "We need this investigation ended."

A puzzle piece clicked into place.

They didn't want the case solved; they wanted it ended. I smirked. Told them they might get further with a bureaucrat than a detective.

"We would never sink that far into the Pit," Greenie said, offended by the idea of working with a politician. "Besides, Hart was the mayor of Hornytown. Know anyone with enough oomph to stop that train?"

I bit back a retort. Couldn't argue it would take a lot more string pulling than a puppet could manage to flip the death of Hornytown's mayor into a cold case. Greenie waited a beat. Then, satisfied by my silence, filled me in on what I didn't know.

The biggest clue was the lack of hoopla. After the killing, no one ordered a lockdown, imposed a curfew, or put any restrictions on the demons or their tourist trade. Sure, a few tourists fled town but as for chaos someone sold Connors the Brooklyn Bridge.

"Got it," I said when they finished. "Ignore the foreground. This case is about the empty space not the painting."

Greenie's balloon-face let out a squee of helium and I spied a smile that made me wonder if their previous brush-off was an act, a test to see if I was going through the motions. They needed to know if . . . Well, they needed to know. I followed their cue and left my emotions locked in my toiletry bag. Told them what I needed.

"We left my Manischewitz stash in the Echo. Had to abandon it. Won't feel comfortable investigating with just a few water balloons."

Urrie looked uneasy, but Greenie agreed to get the super soaker. That settled, I asked my ex-cardplaying pal for some working capital. "Something tempting enough to loosen lips but not so sweet that it raises suspicion."

Urrie agreed to collect some sins for me, but I shook my head.

"You're not going anywhere. If Mortalville's after you, it's only because Hornytown spread the word that you're wanted."

At the directive, tears welled up in Urrie's eyes and something squished in my stomach. Instinct ordered me to comfort her. Sense advised me to distance myself fast. I chose the middle ground and stood there like a schlump. After a minute of saying nothing, I returned to the furry recliner and yawned.

I had no intention of sleeping, but I guess my old card crew joeyed the lemonade. I nodded off wondering why. Wondering what the hell I'd gotten myself into.

8.

I woke up alone. A swing through the cardroom showed nothing disturbed, no signs of a struggle, so I guess she didn't listen to me. In case she was near, I called out her name. No one answered. With no one babysitting me, I got to work.

Behind a sequoia-colored closet door, a walk-in wardrobe held racks of costumes fit for a burlesque. They came in all sizes and lengths. Ranged from see-through-chiffon to the solid-fluff of cotton candy. Some costumes were gorgeously Rubenesque while some of the other size zero and minus three shamatas were barely the size of my hands. The garments brought to mind peek-a-boo cabarets and good times. I chuckled, remembering some of the outfits Greenie wore between sets.

To be clear, neither the dances nor the getups were sinful. Beauty, attraction, and imagination have nothing to do with soul rot. They can, however, be used to raise up true natures. With this in mind, I sought my own costume. I needed to listen to some chatter before a Hart nark marked me and decided the tourist look trumped my usual dick chic.

After a bit of rummaging in the lost and found bin, I chose an orange Hawaiian shirt full of palm trees and winking pineapples. The design even included some panda bears for no reason whatsoever. As I stripped, the buttons on the shirt faded from gold to brass. Meant something. Greenie might tell me if I asked. That is, if they didn't freeze me out for going AWOL. When I finished, I checked out my reflection in a beer stein.

I looked dumpy and eager. The only thing missing was a Minolta around my neck. I practiced some *doe-eye* and some *Look at me! I'm a sucker for any game* expressions. Smirked, and with some false bravado flipped my collar up.

"Looking good, boychik," I said with a wink, then left the wardrobe to work the streets.

—

Outside, a broadside of smells cannonballed into me. Mostly sulphur, bitters, sours, and sweets best described as cloying. Strawberry dominated. Not the fruit, but that awful artificial candy crap. Atop every surface, like a volcanic spew, cigarette ash settled. I covered my nose and wished I had packed a mask.

Hornytown might not kill you, but overexposure would surely be hell on your lungs.

This early in the night (my Faux-lex's sparkly little hand pointed to the two), things were still hopping. A gaggle of tourists flashed selfies every time they neared a billboard or busker. Twirling and strutting, I sauntered towards the Glamourtown District. There, under shadowed awnings, demons dressed in leathers blew kisses, and offered freebies.

I sidled up to one.

"Hey Margie," I breathed. Just five minutes in and my voice croaked like Urrie's.

"Wise guy?" Marge did a double take. Put a hand over his heart. "That really you? Never thought to see you again."

I hushed him.

"Keep a lid on it, Marge. I'm working a case and just thought I'd say 'hi.'"

He gave me a slap on the fanny and I blushed like I always did. Moving a step closer, his nostrils breathed me in to get a measure of how rich the stew of my sins had gotten. I considered asking if I was ready to be taken off the burner but stopped myself. Marge is a working stiff, a cambion half-demon and not a succubus, so with him what you see is what you get. He didn't particularly love his job, got it as a legacy from his dad. Once he confessed to me that he had hoped to become an accountant. Thought that was where the big payday, the lottery-level sins were. He did well enough as a doorman, but his heart was never in it. It kind of hurt to still see him here doing this shtick instead of what he really wanted. I didn't say anything about it though. Who am I to salt a wound?

"Oh Sol, I thought you were done with us after . . ."

I cut him off.

"Things change, bluebell." I shimmied against the brick to make him laugh. A passing crowd mocked me as a newb. After the group entered one of the parlors, I straightened up, faced Marge, and rubbed my fingers together. His eyes widened. We both knew how he loved to trade in gossip. To further melt his resistance, I batted my eyes and offered him my best lopsided Gomer Pyle smile.

A belly laugh exploded through the alley. After he recovered from it, Marge knocked my hat off, and tousled my hair.

I sneered widely with the cockiness of a dick who realized he still had it.

"You really come back just so I could purr in your ear?"

Lacking the words, I leaned forward 'til our foreheads touched. Marge being Marge was fine with me. Hell, I had it on the best authority that sexual orientation wasn't even a sin. Love's redemptive in all its forms. Bigotry, on the hand, is damnable no matter what pious shape it takes.

I held my head on his for a five count. Damn, he had a high temperature. Probably at least a hundred-fifty. When I couldn't take it anymore, I pulled back. Marge chuckled at the flinch. At the signal my callouses and tolerances had faded.

I used that.

My body language said, *I'm just a yutz. Come on, trust me. I'm not a cop anymore. Not a player.*

He sighed and gave me a lick, tasting the words I didn't have the chutzpah to say. My lips shook like the feet of a diver up on the ten-meter platform for the first time. I tried to jump. I really did, but in the end, even after all those self-improvement books, I guess I was still too much of a shmuck to say what needed to be said.

Still, just because I couldn't say the words didn't mean I had to be a dick. So I drew out a math problem I had prepared for him from my pocket. His eyes glistened. With great effort, I brought the right side of my face up into alignment and gave him a brotherly smile. I meant it, too. Marge was one of the good ones.

Marge stroked his beard. He wore one thick and curly enough to hide a potted fern and gave me one last once-over before saying, "You left a big tab, bubby. I might get in trouble."

"Not looking for anything like that. Just wanted to know the mood on the street. I imagine behind the scenes there are some corks popping."

He blew out hard enough to clear away the tobacco.

"Not looking for anything big, huh? You want the whole megillah."

I covered my mouth to hide a laugh. Gave a shrug. Marge chuckled with me.

"All right," Marge conceded. "One thing, but only one thing. There ain't been no parties in Hornytown. At least none that a working stiff would be invited to. Everyone's on edge as if there's a story that ain't being told and no one knows how it's going to shake down. Worse, it's been a day and no one's moved in to take over or demolish the place."

"Hart's Keep still stands?"

"Name's still on the door." Marge nodded.

"Gives me someplace to look."

Marge reached out. Paused. Retracted his mitt.

"Don't, Sol. This is out of your league. Last time, you ran out, people decided not to collect. This one . . . " He shook his head.

I tucked my thumbs in my Hawaiian shirt, realized the futility of trying to look cool, and shrugged. Told him I'd play it safe and that next time I came around I'd pay for a show.

"Promises, promises," Marge called, then returned to his job of suckering tour groups into his establishment. Usually, all it took was a flash of his hairy leg.

Done, I hoofed it onto the gummy main street. A low-hanging pink cutout of a rhino in a tutu blocked me. I ducked under its mechanized Rockettes-style kick and nosed my way out of the alley ready to sniff out the clue Marge had given me. It wasn't much, but he'd confirmed for me that there had been no power struggle and added the tidbit that no one had even made a move. Next step was obviously to talk to someone who should have made a move and find out why they didn't.

A puff of sulfur got in my way. When it cleared, Marge manifested. I startled.

"Oh Sol," he said, placing a burning hand on my chest, "I don't know how you always get to me. Here. Take this. Don't say I never did anything for you."

I whistled, knowing I was too old a dog to merit a bone. Pinching the card, he had just given me, I read.

"Sinatra's," I said.

Marge's face turned serious. "You got that right, boychik. It's jazz. All this is jazz."

9.

While opium, cocaine, and any range of hallucinogents or hallucinoladies rack up pretty high fines in Hornytown, marijuana fails to raise much demonic dander. Hell, after a day in the Pit punishing the worst of the worst, even a mahog requires something to mellow out.

I reached Sinatra's, a mortal-owned pot shop set up in a gentrified circle now marketed as the "Sin District" about an hour after my reunion with Marge. Back in my day, the dump was only fit for those without enough sin in their bank account to get their dinners comped. Now, with its fresh paint job, neon signage, and Art Deco patio, the place had clearly gone A-list. Wearing pandas and coconuts, I felt underdressed but seeing the hearts engraved onto the patio, I decided to trust Marge. He wouldn't have sent me here without reason.

Facing the door, I opened it and immediately relaxed. The tinkling bell and the crossword puzzler who sang a scat song fit for a tapdancing frog sounded the same. Feeling polite, I hummed a bit of Klezmer back at him. With an incline of the head, the puzzler warned me that they weren't partial to any mortal blues here.

I played it cool.

"Haven't worn that drek in so long that the lieutenant took back the uniform," I said and swept past a curtain of crystals that jangled in tune with my chakra. Inside, I nearly tripped over a giggling group of tourists playing Twister and sidled my way towards the counter. On the way, I noticed that the graffiti on the wall wasn't a solo act. Someone had engraved hearts on the walls, tables, chairs, and sandwich board. It made Sinatra's look like a hangout for lovers, except none of the hearts bore any initials inside them. I frowned with such distaste that the crystals clanged with dissonance.

The sound brought out the proprietor real quick.

Jamal Sinatra was a slender Black man in his mid-forties. In his left hand, he held a long, hand-rolled doobie propped up by a silver stick that looked like a tree root gone glam. Over his right shoulder hung a pristine tie-dyed shirt featuring a pattern of concentric rainbow hearts. Something about it caught my eye. I couldn't shake the feeling that the shmata was ill-fitting. A designer rag not even good enough to wipe dishes with.

We frowned at the same time, but Jamal spoke first.

"Start harmonizing. Stop harshing," Jamal Sinatra said, then recognized me and personalized. "Wise Guy, this shop don't need your tsuris."

I rolled up the pineapples on my sleeves in a show of muscle that was more impressive back in my thirties, then picked up a folding menu. Sinatra's boasted ninety-nine varieties of brownies. Midthought I changed tacs, figuring a pot shot deserved a slow roll.

I ordered a Blondie and a Dagwood. The blondie was for the high. The Dagwood was for the munchies. With a sleight of hand that fooled no one, I pretended to take a bite, but slid the blondie into the happy hands of a twenty-something who'd looked like she'd never leave Sinatra's if she had her way.

Jamal rolled his eyes at me and said, "After the laws changed in Mortalville, I figured that the novelty of blazing would wear thin, but it's just the opposite. No one's worried anymore that a toke'll be the thing that tips them into the Pit."

"Laws and hell," I smirked, "don't have much to do with each other."

Sinatra puffed in my face. Smelled expensive, but I coughed it out. Needed a clear head more than a free ride.

"Law's more full of sin than any Hornytown dirt, Wise Guy. Why're you back on the beat? I figured you retired."

I studied him. Wanted to get this right. Jamal was a long-time transplant who moved to Hornytown to get away from the standard bigotry of the mortal world. Kept saying there were more good people here and that the lack of ambiguity appealed to him. At least that was his line back in the day. He seemed more prosperous now, which probably meant he wasn't as happy. I flicked a crystal. Took a bite of my Dagwood. Damn, it was good. I wondered if it was laced with something. Decided I didn't care.

"Jamal," I said.

"Sinatra," he corrected.

"Sinatra," I agreed. "Marge told me you might have some kind words for me."

Jamal whooped and executed a spin move fit for a Heisman-winning halfback then dove onto a bean bag that floated forward to catch him like it was Goku's cloud. Settled, levitated, and high as hell, Jamal wiggled his fingers at me like it was my turn to dance. Being at a pot shop I figured it was only right to start blunt.

"You doing any business at Hart's Keep these days?"

His eyes shot around the room. I marked the locations. Sighed. So much for the engravings being graffiti.

"Protection racket?" I asked, hoping.

His bean bag popped, sprayed pintos all over the room. I rubbed the spot where one hit me, pretty sure the thing would leave a welt.

"What are you accusing me of, Wise Guy. You know better than that. You know better than to bring up that motherfucker in my place."

I held up my hands. but his 'the duchess doth protest too much' bit let me know I was on the right track.

"Easy, friend. It's not an accusation. I'm not even officially here."

The word "friend" got his dander up. His fist clenched. Jamal hated the Mortalville police. Everyone did.

"Better not be," Jamal said and snapped his fingers to summon an imp with a whisk broom. Swishing loudly, the dust devil began to clean the place. I waited until the tautness in Jamal's neck faded, then waited a few more, then apologized. Twice.

"Let's start over," I tried, "I don't have my bearings yet. Thought you could help me."

"You first."

"Fine," I said. "Want to let you know that you overreacted. Could be the supply. Could be you're involved in something you didn't mean to get into. In any case, if an on-duty blue boy saw you freak out to a question that innocent, they'd bring you in for answers. After roughing you up a bit first."

Jamal unslung his tye-die and dropped it on the counter like a ref throwing a flag. I covered my punim with my hands, embarrassed. I deserved a fifteen-yard penalty. I'd been caught cop-splaining. Luckily, Sinatra didn't throw me out of the game.

"That's mortal world shit," he said, dismissively. But he sounded worried like he wasn't sure that the torture in Hornytown was reserved for the condemned anymore. I leaned back onto a stool. Perched like I had no care in the world.

"I'm not going to press," I said, "but someone's hanging on the ledge. I want to help. Wouldn't mind helping you either . . . for old time's sake."

Jamal came close, said to the side of my face, "You really don't want to get involved. This ain't a thing for the Wise, Sol."

The use of my name shook me.

"I'm one of the good ones," I reminded him.

"You were," Jamal allowed. "You cleaned up little messes. Kept some assholes away, but you also ran when things actually got hot. So no, Sol, I don't trust you. Not in this. If you need me to, I'll swear on my supply that I got shit to do with what happened to Hart, but really that's all you're going to get out of me. Officially, I don't know nothing. Now, do us all a favor, Wise Guy and go back to your Silver Spring flat. This isn't a job for Chewbacas and it's certainly not a job for a dick."

I waited a beat, nodded, rose, and headed to the door. Sinatra packed so much into his flow that I'd need a rap sheet to figure it out. As I parted the crystal curtain, I glimpsed Jamal erasing me with his arms crossed across his chest. I shook my head.

I took a last bite of the Dagwood before I started to open the door. Damn it was good. The mutton was so lean and the tomato . . . Double damn! For old times I asked, "You sure you got this covered, Sinatra?"

He nodded. "Hornytown will take care of it. Every bell gets rung in the end."

10.

Back in Greenie's dressing room, I unbuttoned my Hawaiian shirt and rubbed some water on my face. My hair still carried the tobacco reek of my bubby's apartment. The others hadn't returned yet. Needing to distract myself, I shuffled a deck a few times and dealt out a hand of solitaire. As I played, I readied myself to face the music. Not only had I gone AWOL, but I had stayed out way past my bedtime. To avoid the kvetching and as much tsuris as possible I improvised a few believable spiels and strategized on how best to shmooze them, but after playing it out I rejected each of them. As a rule, it's better to stick to the truth with demons. Lies make them salivate and I'm already prime brisket.

Urrie entered, gave me a look like a dogsitter in a panic over a runaway mutt. The relief pleased me. The fury less so. Like she was the cop and I was the perp, I made no move just kept my palms flat on the table in front of me. To my surprise, I wasn't the first thing on her mind.

"Everyone pretended they didn't see me. Didn't know me," the succubus said, lava pooling in her eyes. "No one's got my back."

I flipped a card that I knew would lead nowhere. Wished there was a way to unbury the three.

"Words don't always tell you the story," I soothed, eyes trained on my losing hand. "There's always a tell in the body language. The rhythm of speech. The carriage of the posture. I bet you just misread the room."

"That what your tour of Hornytown taught you?"

I nodded, "That and a few other things, like how many circles got tagged while I was out. Everyone's wearing a Hart on their sleeve these days."

Greenie swung the door open. It banged against the jamb. When they saw me they stopped and dropped a duffle bag on the floor. It plopped with a heavy thump and a tiny slosh. Surprise lit my features, but they weren't done. From a side pocket, they removed my lost Chai and with a demon hot pinch fused the chain's broken links together.

The right side of my face rose to match the left as they handed my life back to me.

"You came back," Greenie said. I couldn't tell if the droplets tasted of relief or sarcasm.

I felt verklempt, overwhelmed and shyly avoided their eyes. "I can't believe you found it."

"We don't break The Ten in Hornytown," Urrie stated, then added, "You have a good time while we were gone?"

Okay, me first. Fair enough.

I described what I discovered during my outing and how I thought the puzzle pieces fit together, ending with, "Pretty sure this is a deeper play than just getting rid of Ronald Hart."

"Bigger than offing the Unicorn?" Urrie asked.

I nodded.

"The goons sent to take me out back at my place weren't prepared for Urrie. Didn't come looking for her." Greenie, frustrated by my poor cardplaying, shoved me aside and won my unwinnable game in six moves. I continued, unfazed. "Pretty sure the pishers were hired to eliminate friends of Hornytown. And if they worked their way down to my name on the list a lot of others have already been crossed out."

"Hard to believe anyone still thought of you as part of Hornytown," Urrie said, "It's been twelve years."

"Seven," Greenie corrected, never one to allow a wrong number through the door.

"Yeah," I admitted. "My resolution slipped once when . . . Anyway, it didn't feel like home so I stayed clear after that. Doesn't matter. I figure for them to go after me means they were running out of friends to discourage or bribe. Also means whoever is behind this isn't afraid to take their show on the road."

"So," Urrie said, refocusing us, "what do you think this is really about?"

"Pretty sure this is a Monopoly play? Someone who wants to own the bank. Put their name on every property."

Urrie tapped her chin, shook her head, as if I'd chosen the wrong board game. "No, that can't be it. No one cares about money in Hornytown."

I swung towards her. Her face gave off hints of Benedict Cumberbatch and Angela Lansbury from her Auntie Mame days.

"Everyone expects a mortal to expire," she continued. "That's why despite the murders, abductions, and the fact that he broke all ten of The Ten no one rose up against him. We just figured Hart was adding to his sin ledger."

"Except," I said, scooping up some candy from a bowl, "I

bet no one's seen Hart in the Pit yet. And everyone's still frozen wondering why."

Midgame, Greenie stopped. When they resumed they ignored the clear path to victory in favor of a more convoluted route. Then one play before winning, took the ace and placed it in my breast pocket.

I blushed. It'd been a long time since someone I respected thought of me as anything other than a joker. The compliment turned me a shade of red equal to a Hornytown local. Then, they added another one.

I looked up, still feeling the weight of the thing that drove me away from Hornytown lurking in the shadow. I forced myself to meet their eyes.

"Hell's eternal; shit between friends doesn't have to be." Greenie nodded. "Always liked the way you play, Sol. You work the room and not the hand."

I sifted some Skittles from one hand into the other. The candy melted.

"So," I asked, "you really think I can do this?" It was an acknowledgement that I was years off my smalltime best.

"While you were out," Greenie updated, waving off my admission of insecurity, "the mayor's office agreed to extradite Urrie. They're saying since it was a mortal killing, mortal justice has to take the lead."

"They raised," I noted.

I turned towards Urrie. Sweet-faced as Gidget, subtle as Betty Boop.

"They're asking for the death penalty, Sol. The death penalty."

The room chilled. My M&Ms shuddered. The licorice whips tied themselves in knots. Every fakakta piece of candy in the dish exhibited distress except the Red Hots.

I hate those bastards.

"Death," I repeated. "Is that even possible?"

The demons shared a moment before nodding.

I felt verklempt. Demon immortality stands as one of the bedrocks. With Hornytown's emergence rewriting so many of the rules, this at least had been a surety. In my life there had been four things I could be sure of: Death, Taxes, and you couldn't outlast the demon assigned to your sin ledger. The fourth? I'm keeping that in my back pocket. You don't have to know everything.

I reached out to comfort the succubus in front of me, not as one of the seduced but like someone who actually meant it. Her expression . . . just for a moment changed. Gone was the forced sexiness. In its place something beautiful blossomed. I rocked back, too startled to comment, then it hit me.

Around here, knowledge fetched a higher price than a tissue Michael Jackson had sneezed into.

"Greenie," I said, cutting the deck. "We need a seat at the table. To make our next play we need to rub shoulders with some high rollers. Do you still—?"

The puppet measured me, executed a trick shuffle. Then, smiled over their shoulder and said, "Yeah, I know a place."

11.

I drew four, signaling the constancy of my luck. Greenie checked. Urrie raised. Four other demons sat around the table. Their heat made me sweat more than the stakes. To my left, a big pharma CEO chomped down on a cigar, while the greasy North Dakota oil magnate dabbed his head. Each demon, including my cardplaying pals, wore a smile.

"So, pigeon?" a red-spiked bruiser asked. "You going out yet?"

I studied my cards. To my surprise, the hand matched my face. I held a flush. Sadly, my pile of chips failed to meet the minimum. Like a minnow in a bay of poker-sharks, I glanced at my hand and pile and then back at my hand. I started to fold, but baring their puppet teeth, Greenie baited the hook by reminding me I could trade info for cash. The other demons agreed fast as a blink. After all, knowledge and sin have been known to flirt like Romeo and Juliet. I sighed like I was considering Greenie's offer.

No one expected me to tell the truth, the whole truth, and nothing but the truth. We were playing poker after all, but my cardplaying pal appreciated the taste of a good truth almost as much as a salacious lie. I chose to share a truth.

"Identical twins lack the same fingerprints," I shared to raised eyebrows. "Learned that one while chasing a certain set of cat-burgling brothers. You see, every time they worked a job, one of 'em made sure to show off their punim. For years, they kept getting away with their crimes because the physical evidence always contradicted the eyewitness reports."

I figured that'd be juicy enough to keep me in the game. My trivia had the advantage of being true as well as being sin adjacent. Before that, I popped off about birds to make the ante. Never met a demon who didn't fixate on wings and the mechanics of natural flight.

When the conversion rate was given, Big Pharma didn't take it too well.

"Identical twins?" he groused. "Who the fuck gives a rat's ass about identical twins. I'm leaking prime insider info here. Shit'll make you a fortune on the stock market."

The demons shushed him. Big Pharma had already lost more than me. Lost more than I'd made in my whole life, but he hadn't learned his lesson yet. I guess it takes a while for some mortals to learn not to bluff. Especially the ones who make their livelihood off of lies.

"Being able to differentiate people who otherwise escape notice might hold a certain attraction to those who haunt Hornytown." I shrugged. "Me, I cue more on body language, dialect, little mannerisms, but it might be a comfort finding out how to ID a perp who can change their face."

The glamoured demons took that extra bit as a call and raise. Some of them had a tough time distinguishing each other. I caught Urrie's eyes. With her description postered around town she wore a different face. To the group, she had introduced herself as Yuri and responded to the name so naturally you'd think she'd worn it her whole life. For a moment, I wondered if she had. Decided it didn't matter. What mattered was staying in the game long enough to grift some info from the sucker seated next to me. To stay in the hand, I tossed in another secret.

Big Pharma folded. Stormed out. The rest called. I lost to a full house. Sixes over nines. I downed some more comped fire water.

Greenie had promised a Hart. Said they liked to slum it after a striptease and this was one of their preferred haunts. Fitting with my luck, the best that showed up was some backroom knob wearing a Hart-studded earring and a company uniform. The schlimazel kept slamming his hand down after every deal. By the third round, he started accusing the demons of dealing from the bottom of the deck. Claimed Greenie was counting cards. After several more rounds of threats, they cut him off from the fire water.

He scowled. Glowered at his chips. His stack imitated an anthill. Seizing the opportunity, I nudged him with my elbow.

"I could bump you some info," I offered, friendly-like.

He brightened.

He was one of those guys, who when they fell behind, always doubled down. Never realized that the acceleration of a fall held the same for poker as it did for Newtonian apples. Told me he could arrange some freebies as a thank you. Asked me if I'd ever taken advantage of the suite life.

I told him I hadn't.

With stars in my eyes, I slid him some details that hadn't made it out of some decade-old case files. Juicy stuff. Naughtier than the stuff I'd laid down. Things which proved the guilt of some people too powerful to be prosecuted.

"Oh. That's good," he said. Laughed when after hearing it, Yuri folded with a bitter, "Too rich for my blood."

He caught on. I fed him a few more scraps that helped fuel a little winning streak. The newfound chips lubricated his lips better than booze. But good things come to an end and hand by hand, he found his pile shrinking. When he was all but busted again, he looked at me hopefully, but I slid my hand in a "no more" gesture and told him I had to keep some shit in reserve.

"You think you're the only one who knows stuff?" the schlimazel said. I tilted my head in a way that expressed doubt. "You think I'm bluffing."

Here it comes.

"Keep this to yourselves, okay," he began. "Only a select few inside the Keep know this, but the day Hart got it . . ." Better sense caused him to look around the room, but so many of us had already spilled our guts that he felt safe. He thought he had shit to blackmail us for years. "The day Hart got it, no one called a doctor. No one rang for an ambulance. Hell, no one even called a janitor to clean up the mess."

"Shit," I said.

"Yeah," the schlimazel agreed. "At first I thought they were trying to keep things quiet. That Junior didn't want anyone knowing, but . . ." and his voice dropped even lower, "but the orders weren't coming from Junior. All them vipers and no one made a play. You know what that means."

He leaned back, tented his fingers behind his head. Smug.

We gave him our coins, our promise to stay mum, and kvelled about how fortunate we felt to be in the graces of such a person-in-the-know. When the door slammed, my eyes bugged. The idea in my head was so meshuggeneh I knew it had to be true. Greenie started to say something, but I raised a hand, took my phone out of my pocket and speed dialed.

"Connors," I said into the receiver. The lieutenant's answer was so loud every demon in the room flinched. I waited her out and after she finished said in a stone-dead voice, "When can you get here? We got to meet."

12.

Connors arrived at the lakeside diner wearing her civies: black skirt, floral blouse, and a handbag big enough to count as a carry-on. She spotted me before the host could ask her how many were in her party. As she strode my way, she stroked the silver heart locket at her neck like it was Van Helsing's cross. She tried to play it cool, but with her eyes cartoon-wide she fooled no one. When she reached the table, instead of sitting, she dug into her handbag to remove a sanitizer.

Spritz. Wipe. Spritz. Wipe. Spritz. Wipe. It took three goes to clean her side of the booth to her satisfaction. The wait staff took no offense. They'd seen it before.

"I don't like 'off the books' meetings, Sol." She spoke before offering a nod or handshake. Wanted to exert control in a place she felt out of control.

"Didn't feel I had a choice," I said, spinning my fedora on a finger and ordering us both a slice of pie.

Our server, an androgynous imp, nodded and placed a handful of wet naps on the table for the Lieutenant but shook off Connors' request for coffee.

"It's mostly psychological, honey," the imp said, "but that doesn't make the effect any less real. Chamomile is better for the nerves."

Connors repeated her order, then she propped her elbows on the table and waited a beat. The imp caught the cue and departed to warm our pie, saying they'd be back to check on us after we had a chance to chat. I watched them go. Part of me wanted to call the server back and change Connors's order to devil's food cake, but I needed the lieutenant on my side so I abstained from the wise guy bit.

When we were finally alone, Connors reminded me that I had brought her here because I said I had some information. I told her I had a theory. She responded with a look. I conceded the point. I wasn't here to fight. I was here to recruit.

Underneath the table, I folded and refolded my napkin. Maybe she'd actually come to listen, but I doubted it. Hornytown was not only out of her comfort zone; it was out of her jurisdiction. I released a breath and chose to go all in.

"I found Urrie," I said.

At the mention of the sheyd, her eyes shrank to slits and her expression grew so severe I half-expected steam to flare from her nostrils. As I suspected, Connors had been given a name, not just a description.

"When?"

I twiddled my thumbs, weighing white lies. I settled on earlier today. Not exactly true, but only twenty-four hours off.

"And you got her to agree to surrender herself?"

The coolness in her demeanor made me want to spill the beans. Give up Urrie's confidence. But spilled beans do nothing but give you a case of the runs, so I bit my lip and continued origami-ing under the table.

"The reward . . ."

"Is damn high. Hart's heirs are rumored to be making a

statement soon that no one gets away with hurting one of their own."

"The reward is something I'm not interested in."

I was glad our drinks hadn't arrived yet. Connors' spurt of laughter would have rained all over me. As it was, I felt myself go red from embarrassment instead of scalding chamomile. I started over.

"I'm not here to negotiate about money."

The degree to which Connors arched her eyebrow put her at risk of a sprain.

"She's a client then. And you're here to betray her? What? This your moment to get your thirty silver coins?"

I got the reference from a Webber and Rice musical, but before I could say anything, she apologized. Accusing Sol Weiss of being Judas is an Inquisition too far.

The pie arrived. Mexican hot chocolate for her and quince for me. I tapped the edge of my mug and the imp refilled it with a hard cider that smelled of first knowledge. Connors tried again for coffee. From the back, I saw Urrie peek her head out of the kitchen door. And Connors, being good at what she does, turned around at the slight shake of my head.

"So, she's here," Connors said.

It wasn't a question.

"She didn't do it," I said.

"Then tell her to come forward."

I didn't. Also didn't say that we both knew plenty of cases where the verdict was decided well before the jury was picked or that some cases ended with accidental police violence. She heard every word I didn't say. Neither of us were rookies.

She spooned up a forkful of pie. So did I.

"What makes you think she didn't do it?" Connors broke the pause. "Make it good."

I dabbed the corner of my smirk with my torn napkin. Noticed her noticing how I'd nervoused the paper to pieces.

"I can't tell you that until we come to an agreement."

"Then I can't do much, can I?" Took a few bites. Waited for her puppy to break. I didn't.

"Why call me, Sol? We were never close. You don't have any favors to call in. Why make the call?"

My eyes surveyed the diner. In a normal sting, Connors would have half the place filled with plainclothes. Maybe even set up a sniper. That could still be the case. She wouldn't have called up any blues I knew.

Around my pie I mumbled, "Problem with this case is there's no victim. Ronald Hart isn't dead."

"You know this?"

"I suspect . . ."

"Fuck me, Sol. Do better."

To my surprise, she brought out her phone. Showed me several shots of Ronald Hart. Whoever went at the body did it with extreme prejudice. Fingers bitten off. Neck slashed. Teeth and jaw gouged out. Body bald and burned like he'd been tossed in the Pit. I reached for the phone. Tweezered with my fingers to zoom in.

Damn.

I studied the picture. Went to the next one. Focused hard on that one, too. While I did, Dennis the freaking

Menace showed up at our table to ask how we liked our pie. Automatically, I thanked them.

Their voice hadn't changed. The eagerness in our imp server's stride was the same. I was getting to know them well enough that I might recognize them the next time I saw them on the street. Most mortals can't do that, but I had the knack. I had the—

"If I look at this photo," I began, hoping my brain would catch up with my tongue, "I see someone taken out by someone with a Pit profile. But Urrie is a seducer, not a torturer."

"Also, look at the fingers."

"What fingers?"

"Right. They're missing. No fingerprints."

My brain shook hands with my tongue. My tongue didn't lash me for taking so long. I appreciated its forbearance.

"And the missing teeth? No dental records. The hair. No DNA."

"We can get DNA from blood, spit, or skin, Sol." But her voice held a trace of doubt.

"Hmm," I said, "I bet no one from the mayor's office delivered a body to the coroner? All you got are these pictures, right?"

It was a guess, but a good one. One confirmed by a look of exasperation. So I continued talking.

"Whoever killed the person in this photo either really hated Hart or wanted to make sure no forensics team would be able to ID him."

Her brow creased. She chewed her pie slowly.

"Sol," she said after reexamining the photos, finally. "It doesn't fly. The Mayor's office didn't need to cooperate at all."

My tongue poked my cheek, suddenly less happy with my brain.

Forcing a cough to stall for time, I downed some cider. She laughed at me and pushed her half-finished plate in my direction.

"What matters is what we can prove. What we think doesn't matter." Connors leaned forward. "Don't let an attractive client fog your brain."

We both examined our cards. I thought hers were better. I decided to pull an ace from my sleeve before we played show and tell.

"Pretty exciting, isn't it?" I leaned in close as if shedding a mask. "If this goes as planned and DC convicts, we get to find out how to kill one of them."

To her credit, she kept it cool. Even looking for a tell, I didn't see anything except maybe a little extra twinkle in her eye.

"There's no death penalty in DC. Federal cases are pretty rare. Bring her out, Sol."

I measured the thaw. Didn't find any.

I sagged. Always figured I'd have to go all in. Greenie told me as much.

"Okay, you win." I turned and waved. "Urrie."

Connors' smirk reminded me of mine. It was eerie.

We waited.

Marilyn Monroe, Beyoncé, and my first high school crush all wrapped up in one sauntered out. At least that's what I saw, but not Connors. From her double, triple, and quadruple take, I knew she saw someone else.

Before I could correct her, she slapped her locket. It cracked with a snkkt and a waft of powder. Then, she lunged at Urrie.

In three strides, she reached the demon, spun her around, and pulled her arm behind her back. To my shock, Urrie struggled. It wasn't possible. A mortal attempting to restrain a succubus should have been about as effective as a six-year-old tackling a linebacker.

"Easy, Connors," I cautioned.

Her locket pendulumed and metronomed. Dust radiated out of it. The pieces rotated like the debris around Saturn. She sniffed up another noseful.

I sighed. As a vice cop, I'd heard about this, but I'd never seen it in person. Connors was strung out on horn.

"This isn't her," Connors raged. "Who is this? It's not even a woman. Where's the bitch that offed the Unicorn?"

Despite the nearest four tables suddenly emptying out, I relaxed a hair. The shout at least confirmed that Connors was Connors and not a doppelganger, but just to be sure, I quick-drew a water balloon I'd secreted in my overcoat and doused her with a dose of Manischewitz.

The low caliber wine splashed off her cheek and stained her blouse, but didn't faze her. Now, 11% alcohol isn't enough to knock out a full demon, but I've never seen one not shuffle back a step or two from the sting. I tried to say something to placate Connors, but before I got the words out, glass crashed around our heads.

Six bespoke figures entered the scene, each wearing their own locket. It was my turn for a double take. I guess I had known it all along, but I didn't want to believe. Connors wasn't wearing a heart. She was wearing a Hart. My mouth fell open, but before I could curse her out, a familiar face stepped forward.

"Pinstripes?" I said, stumbling back.

"Don't let the Wise Guy get away," Pinstripes said, rushing me. "Bastard owes me a car."

Before he got to me, our server, taking exception to a Nazi in their diner, 'accidentally' clocked him with a frying pan, then backhanded him with a spatula. Pinstripes howled in rage. Not finished, the imp mooned him.

As the imp led Pinstripes on a merry chase, I turned my attention back to Connors. No recognition lingered in her steroid-rage filled eyes. "Give me the succubus!" she roared, unaware that she held her target beneath her knee in an armlock. "I want her now!" Spit spraying from her mouth, her rant continued. "You're going down. All of you. I'm taking you in. You're all going to the Keep!"

I grabbed two more water balloons out of my overcoat and held them high. A goon fired what probably wasn't a warning shot an inch away from my head. I flipped a table. Hid behind it. From my knees, I caught sight of the goon's black Testonis. A pair of shoes like that cost twice a cop's annual salary. With a semicircle of bespoke goons pressing me, Connors' words struck home.

"Keep?" I asked. "You mean station, don't you?"

Everyone in the diner, goon and imp, stopped as the import

of Connors' slip hit home. Even Pinstripes, face mashed with pie and a spritz of seltzer an inch from his punim, froze. Taking control of the moment, I stood up from behind my upturned table and challenged my ex-lieutenant to admit the truth.

"Who is it, Connors? Who you working for?"

"This doesn't have to get messy," a new voice said in the middle of our food fight. My eyes flicked to the front door as a very punchable face strode towards us.

I recognized him from the press conferences, from the social media clips, from the stubble and disoriented eyes. My mouth formed the name he hated to be called.

"Junior."

The bastard surveyed the diner with disdain. Hands on his lapels, his smirk out-tilted mine by a long shot. When he spoke, his voice carried the nasal blah-blah-blah of the eternally self-entitled.

"As a duly appointed officer of the mayor's office working in conjunction with the DCPD, I order you to surrender yourselves now."

On the diner tables, all the baked potatoes eyed each other. The corn on the cob, all ears, popped off. In their salad bowls, leaves of lettuce lost heart and wilted. In the end, it was Urrie who acted. Seeing Junior must have been too much for her.

Still pinned by Connors, she twisted her hand one hundred and eighty degrees and stabbed Connors through the sole of her flats with her claws. Then, she tickled Connor's arch.

Okay, tickle is underselling it. Fingers flicking fast as a world-class typist, she did some kind of nerve-tap-dance-acupressure. When the typewriter dinged, Connor's eyes rolled up.

I smirked. Never mess with a succubus.

Getting into the action, Greenie unloaded a cleaver into the breast jacket of a demon. They staggered, then realized that mortal blows were for mortals and tossed the puppet into a wall. Pinstripes finally got a hold of our server. Me, behind the shelter of my table and with Manischewitz in hand, finally decided to stand up.

I wound up and threw a strike at the nearest sheyd. The brachot inside the latex water balloon released. As the Kosher wine did its work, the demon's teeth dripped out of their mouth like hot fudge.

Like a bully who knew bupkes about pain, the goon fell to his knees and shrieked as if his world was ending. The cry turned every head. Shock ran through the diner. A demon was hurt. A demon was down. And the mensch who did it had another water balloon.

"Anyone else!" I bluffed, "I'll kiddush you straight into the Pit."

Junior retreated. Once he was safely behind a wall of goons, he threatened us again. I decided that was a good time to mock him.

"Hart's in the Pit," I said. "You don't have authority here anymore."

He acted like no one had ever stood up to him before. Probably because no one ever had. Red-faced, he jumped up and down. Gave me what I needed.

"Shut up!" he tantrummed. "You don't know nothing. The Unicorn still rules this joint."

It was all I needed. Connors couldn't deny what that blurt

meant ... unless she was fully bought which, I sighed, she probably was.

Realizing what he'd said, Junior ordered his goons to go all Sixth on our tucheses. When they balked, he said he didn't care about The Ten. He wanted us dead. Calmly, I signaled Greenie. With a nod, they manifested my duffle and flipped me my super soaker.

Ta-tump. Ta-tump. Ta-tump.

My pumping told everyone in the room, I had plenty of Manischewitz in the canister. I was locked, loaded and ready to spritz.

"Connors!" I said, "You heard Junior. My client is innocent. Time to go home."

Her head swiveled towards me. The yellowing of her sclera indicated the horn dust was washing out. As she rose, the legs beneath her skirt looked unsteady. To my disappointment, she doubled down.

"Solomon Weiss, put your hands up," she said. "You're under arrest for interfering with an official investigation."

I shook my head. Said, "I'm not asking for a mitzvah, Alfreda. I'm asking you to do the right thing."

My glare must have held something in it because Connors flinched. She didn't know there were lines I'd never cross so she tried one more time.

"This could have been so much cleaner. We could have shared the reward. Think about what you're doing. Jews don't even believe in Hell. Why fight for someone your people don't believe in?"

When she saw my back stiffen, she grew more desperate.

"Sol, You're working for the Devil. We have to take DC back. God damn it, we have to break the circle."

I whistled. It took guts to blaspheme in Hornytown. Seeing me distracted, Junior's goons edged forward. I decided they needed to know I wasn't bluffing.

Four got it in their worsted wool. Now, hitting cloth ain't the same as hitting skin, but it taught them I was serious. To emphasize the lesson, I pumped my soaker hard again. Yeah, I know, it was a dick move, but it worked.

Part of me wanted to stay, to drench them, to . . . ironically baptize them with Kosher wine, but Urrie put a hand on my shoulder—and I knew she was right—so we ran for it.

13.

Edges of corded rope nipped my palms as we descended into the Pit. The pain urged me to let go. Accept the fall I deserve.

After we fled the diner, I'd rejected returning to the dressing room. We needed to go somewhere they wouldn't. Greenie assured us that Hart's goons wouldn't chase us down the glass ladder. All I knew was no cop goes near the Pit. Not for a dare. Not for a pay day. Hornytown was one thing. The Pit was the real deal. Still, safe is a relative thing. Only a few rungs down and my breath tasted of the worst kind of polluted overflow and my sweat boiled off me. Worse, there were no echoes. No cranks. No whips. No crackles of fire. I shivered with the knowledge that some things were so horrible they transcended screams.

Gravity's anchor pulled against me. It dragged with more force than ever before. Into my ear, a trustworthy voice whispered that I belonged here. I shook my head, annoyed that it told me something I already knew.

Besides me, Urrie chanted. Something about not needing to be here again. She was a wrong below me and moving steadily. I shivered. Hated myself for wasting energy.

I slipped. Urrie caught me. It was the second time. The first happened after a smoky miasma porcupined my lungs.

She asked if I was okay and I nodded, but made it only twenty more feet before Urrie announced to the group my bloody hands needed attention. Sarcasm roiled out of me.

"What? You going to call 911? Get a paramedic to the Pit?"

She ignored me as well as the fact that holding still did nothing more than allow the glass to bite deeper. Instead, calmly, she stripped off her hoodie, shredded it, and climbed upwards 'til we shared a rung, then gently wrapped the strips around my hands. It only took a dozen or so more feet before the glass sliced through the cloth, but the gesture stuck with me and I clung to the thought that kindness still existed.

After a time, who knows how long, open mouthed caves with jagged stalactite teeth appeared in the rockface. Urrie encouraged me. Told me all I had to do was make it to them and I'd be okay. I fixated on this goal, focused all my attention on the open mouths even though from one of them, a familiar voice rose to chide me.

"Sol, you got too good an imagination."

"Bubbe?"

I shook away the hallucination. There was no way. Not her. Not here.

"That's why you hurt all the time," Bubbe continued. "Don't feel so much my little shin angela. Let go. All you have to do is let go."

I nodded. She was right.

But life is stubborn, so I kept climbing. Hand over hand. Rung over rung. Wrong after wrong.

My next test came in the form of the mug of a kid I cheap-shotted back in elementary school. A kid I sent to the hospital because my friends dared me and because a little guy has to double prove he's tough enough not to become a target himself. I struggled to remember the kid's name, but all I recalled was that he had invited me to his birthday party and we played Xbox at his house a few times before the incident.

I almost laughed. Of all the reasons I belonged in the Pit, this one seemed slight.

I stole.

I cheated.

I hurt.

I lied.

Each papercut sin sliced deep.

I closed my eyes and . . . *Shawn*.

"There," Urrie interjected. "We're almost there. Trust me, the shadows won't follow there, Sol."

Sounded like bullshit, but I let her strong hands guide me into an open mouth. Just before it swallowed me, I tried to push off, howling that I belonged in the Pit, but those clawed hands rocked me. Kept me from jumping.

I didn't deserve it.

"You're doing well," a smoker's voice said as my tuches was lowered onto a slab. I tried to smile. Felt my lips crack.

"Wa—"

"We'll get you water. Focus on your core. You're a good man, Solomon Weiss. This is not beyond your tolerance. Not this high up."

"You're not getting off that easy," Greenie agreed. "You don't get to run away again. Not even here."

"Mah halo. I lost mah halo. It gun. Where it gun?" To my ears, I sounded drunk.

Greenie sought to distract me by spouting trivia. It was so

like them. They always sought comfort in patter when things got tough. Silly nothings that would barely cover the ante at a poker table.

"We excavated this tunnel," they informed us, "in the 1930s to meet the threat of mass communication."

"It wasn't really a new sin," Urrie said, picking up the thread.

I stared at Greenie's balloon-face and wondered why had I had never asked them their name? Why I had contented myself with this nickname?

Why I always distanced myself from my friends?

In answer to Greenie, Urrie trotted out words like *EIGHT*. Not the number. The Commandment. When they said it, the word wore a capital letter, was italicized, and was written in a bold, echo-y font.

I focused on the arguing. The existence of prattle. Urrie steered the conversation towards historical precedents. Greenie countered with numbers. It reminded me of my family bickering. Led me towards a world of gray.

"Television," Urrie groused, "was worse than radio."

"Radio is pretty bad. Don't you remember—"

"Advertisers," I guessed, trying to become a part of the conversation, to carve out an identity outside of my sins.

"Them too," Urrie said, "but televangelists."

A whoosh of fire sped past the inset we sheltered in.

"Televangelists and internet trolls," Greenie agreed. "Not the deepest part of the Pit. But plenty deep."

An idea sparked. I blew on it, trying to kindle fire.

We had come down here to hide, seeking a place to

regroup. But maybe also because I needed to be here, not because I deserved to burn, but because below us awaited a weapon. I tuned out the discussion of where trolling and bullying fit into the 'Thou shalt nots' and focused on why this reservoir of evil was useful.

And then it hit me who Ronald Hart reminded me of.

More than a businessman and a wannabe mobster. More than a mayor who wanted to rule the roost and a gonif who made people commit unforgivable sins. The Unicorn was a bully with a glass jaw. That is, Ronald Hart could never let an insult go without punching back.

"No one condemned Caesar after his death," I paraphrased. "That's why Hart could pull off his disappearing act. It worked because everyone's still scared of him."

Ashamed, I realized that going to Sinatra's and the diner was an act of avoidance. I should have gone straight to the Keep. That's where the evidence was. The only reason I hadn't was because I was afraid of Hart too.

That had to change. We needed to smoke the Unicorn out. Get under his skin.

"We need verbal Manischewitz," I said aloud, testing out the words.

And I did . . . I knew just the person to deliver it.

"When I was young," I began, "there was this kid."

Each of my demon friends sat up. They stopped debating radio versus TV. They could smell the sin I was about to feed them was full Thanksgiving.

"Her name was Shawn. She was the . . . She was the kind of person who'd size you up and cut you down. One, two, three."

I took a breath, acid already churning in my gut. Just invoking Shawn's name brought me back to middle school. Back then I was a yutz with a rep hanging by a thread and Shawn was the queen who sprinted along every hallway flashing scissors.

"I was never worthy of her notice, but that didn't mean she spared me. She sliced me down whenever I strolled into her sights. At thirteen, she was already so skilled that she never needed to learn a thing about me to destroy me. And she did. Over and over again.

"She was Goliath and I carried no sling.

"Every day, I obsessed on figuring out ways to avoid her. If I heard her in the hallway, I jammed myself into a locker. On the few occasions we shared a class, I never raised a hand. Answered questions wrong when called upon. Anything to avoid her targeting radar.

"And she didn't give a damn about me. My arch nemesis and the biggest boogeyman of my life didn't even know my name.

"I'm not proud of what I did. But early days on the beat, I manufactured some bullshit about her. Whispered that Shawn talked smack about some very bad cats. It was an easy lie to believe. Shawn had a rep. Had already thrown a mountain of corpses under the bus—

"Afterward, my conscience tried to convince me I only wanted her roughed up a bit.

"Ninth that. From the first time I heard what happened to her, I blamed myself for her murder. Sure, it changed me, set me on a straighter road and might be the only reason I'm visiting the Pit today instead of living here. But those are damn selfish silver linings."

I took a deep breath and choked. Pit air is not meant for clearing your head. It's for bringing you full circle. Except these circles ain't stable orbits, they're black holes. They're Charybdis and you're in a row boat.

When I finished my story, my companions looked satiated. Well, I thought, let them feed. This sin didn't deserve to be forgiven. Not ever. I gave Urrie a nod of thanks. She laughed and told me not to thank her tormentors, but I was fixed on the answer the Pit had given me. Standing up I shuffled a step towards the glass ladder. My cardplaying pal held me back.

"I'm not trying to jump," I told them. "I have the answer. She's the answer."

"Shawn?" Greenie asked, then dismissed the idea. "Rumors are soft-core sin."

I shook my head, sure I was onto something.

"Shawn's our joker, Greenie," I said. "If anyone can goad the Unicorn out of hiding, it's her. Maybe giving her a chance to do good would—"

Greenie didn't answer, but leveled their card-shark eyes at me recognizing that I just pushed a whole lot of coins into the center of the table despite only holding a pair of deuces.

Urrie shook her head, "It's impossible. Sentences are firm. There's no lessening for good behavior. Besides, do you really think your personal devil will help you just because you bat your long lashes at her?"

Gravity kept me from smiling so I grabbed Urrie's burning hands with my bleeding ones. "If Shawn gets to Hart.

He'll show his punim . . . If he does that, you walk. We all go home."

"Fume-sick," Urrie snorted.

"Maybe," Greenie said after a moment, "but sometimes you draw an inside straight."

"And that's who Shawn is." I grinned. "A bad-mouthed pebble that starts an avalanche."

Urrie checked both of us out. Measured our conviction. Our lunacy. To her horror, it clicked that we were both card-players. Gamblers. That was who she had pinned her hopes to. Part of me expected her to laugh, come up with a better plan. Maybe even eject me into the Pit, but to my dismay, she went for it.

Well fuckity, fuck, fuck. Time to meet my boogeyman in the deepest Pit of Hell.

14.

Smoke swirled like the plume from a pack of cigarettes eager to reach a gaggle of kids. I blinked away the itch in my eyes, pressed my lids tight to force some moisture into them. This far down, the Pit's gravity pulled so bad on my right side that I felt it creep onto my left. Nothing to do about that. No use worrying that it signaled that my sin-level surpassed the fifty percent mark. I released the glass ladder. It jangled. Full weight, I crashed onto a basalt platform.

"Ummph!" I umphed.

Urrie tied me to her back, complaining that if I could barely walk there was no way I could climb. Once secured, she hopped to test the binding. Her hair whipped me, each strand striking like a dominatrix's whip. Not that I know what that feels like.

Satisfied, she peered over the lip of the platform and a bit of Deuteronomy popped into my head—

You may view the land from a distance, but you shall not enter it.

And I thought, what the fuck is a good boy like me doing here? How far am I willing to fall?

I closed my eyes when Urrie leapt. We freefell several stories before she grasped the glass again. The pressure on my chest grew so severe my breath failed when I tried to inhale. After a beat, she let go again, dropping another hundred yards in a handful of seconds.

Was I really doing this? Was I really putting my life in the hands of a demon? Micah's voice filled my head.

Trust no friend, rely on no intimate, be guarded in speech with her who lies in your bosom. For son spurns father, daughter rises up against mother, daughter-in-law against mother-in-law; a man's own household are his enemies.

We fell again.

It took a minute to realize we'd stopped. The rush and pull of vertigo continued while my cardplaying pals untied me, massaged my muscles. In the reflection of a jagged facet of ebony, I saw that the right half of my face stretched below my collarbone. Beside me, Urrie felt cool.

The thought staggered me.

How hot must it be for Urrie to feel cool!

I tried to walk the place off. Fell forward with an Igor limp. Beneath me, the ground felt chalky and bumpy as a lunar surface. I wanted to kiss it, but the thud of someone that strode with the three-beat staccato of a cane stopped me. With great effort, I lifted my head and saw a hillock whose breath huffed like a furnace. Everything in me cried out, 'Run!' Lucky for me, I never listened to sense.

"What is that?" I wheezed, impressed with myself for being able to squeeze out words. "It smells like cabbage."

"Cruel," the hillock said appreciatively. "I like it."

We waited a beat as he started to shuffle back from wherever he came. Relief flooded through me. Then, he turned to wave a hand at us and said, "Follow me."

Through the haze, I found myself following an old burlap robe plumped by overgrown muscles. The hillock's horns grew slantwise like a steer. They were yellowed from pit smoke. Urrie ran up to him, and the hillock's face lit up like a mother seeing their baby.

"We're here to confront a troll, Bernie," she said.

"Do you think she deserves it?" the hillock answered. "Facing one's murderer. Tch. Usually goes the other way around, you know."

"Different times," Greenie added.

"I suppose."

We went forward. I'd say I walked, but really I was slung between a green puppet and a succubus who now looked vaguely like one of my PE teachers. Every so often, I tried to help by swinging a leg. Ahead of me, I saw my first honest to G . . . A real life Pit torture chamber.

In it, a gob of a human started reconstituting in a vat of acid. His look of despair suggested this melting had happened so many times that he just didn't care anymore. In fact as I started walking by, he began to hum. No wonder the devil thought he needed to upskill his workers. Humans really are so much better at making each other suffer.

"We're here to see . . ." I started.

"I know. I know," Bernie muttered, turning down a shaft of lava. I stumbled. This time I couldn't rise. Urrie swept me up and carried me like a bride being walked across the threshold. I think part of her regretted bringing me into this. Putting me through this. Bernie, on the other hand, ignored my physical distress and just finished what he began to say. "You don't wind up here without reason. You don't get here without our knowing it."

"So you know . . ."

"You don't smell like one of them Hart ambassadors. Nasty bunch, them. Take too many notes. Giggle a lot." Bernie gave me the eye. "Anyone who enjoys the work isn't fit for the job. Remember that, Solomon Weiss."

"No worries," I said softly, "I'm Jewish. We're more about enduring pain than getting off on it."

With a sniff that lifted my feet towards his nose, Bernie measured me. "Guilt, bitterness, regret. A fine mix. Not quite tender enough. Soon though. Soon."

I hardened.

Bernie's laugh echoed through the pits.

15.

In an alcove that looked like the entrance to a Bohemian coffee shop, a group of penitents queued up. One by one they stopped under a spotlight intense as a Death Star laser, pulled out a sheet of paper, and began to recite slam poetry. Few had the knack, but they all put their sins to verse, hoping for snaps, not hisses.

"Welcome to Confession Hall," Bernie chuckled. "Before we make an exception, you need to impress us. Show us your heart, Solomon Weiss."

"Words ain't my preferred ammo," I bluffed, but Bernie just clapped and said, "Good first line."

Neither Greenie nor Urrie attempted to put a stop to this farce as Bernie grabbed me and placed me into the line. At least they offered me some advice: Greenie urged me to concentrate on the meter and Urrie said, "Make it good."

Six people went before me. Or maybe it was six hundred. I don't have an ear for poetry, so I tuned out. All I recognized was that this was a processing line. A confessional before sentencing. Looking at the bright side, I figured not many of us got a practice go before the real thing. As I watched, a demon escorted a poet to a trash chute. Apparently that one did okay because the next one got shunted towards something called the incinerator.

I should have spent my waiting time putting words

together. Maybe stringing together song lyrics that made me misty. Instead, when the spotlight glared in my face, I felt empty. Blank as an unprimed canvas.

Prompted, I grabbed the mic. It whined with feedback. I tapped it.

"Is this thing on?" I asked, earning not a single smile, laugh, or acknowledgment. Guess they heard that one before. Instead of starting, I tried to defer, "Never been a man of words."

"Every soul has poetry in them," Urrie encouraged before getting shushed.

I mumbled something noncommittal and waited for the hook. No words came. I wondered how long they'd give me. Thought back to high school, trying to remember English class. Surely, I'd once matched rhythm to rhyme in a pretty way.

"Words ain't my preferred ammo," I said because you have to say something before they decide you got nothing to say and Bernie liked it when I said it the first time.

"Deeds," I said, and wondered if I was bullshitting myself.

"Boo!" Bernie said. "That's not even haiku. Try some modernist abstract crap."

"Fuck you!" I said under my breath.

"Better," Bernie acknowledged.

All right. If that's what he wanted.

"Words ain't my preferred ammo.
You want my heart? Fuck you. It's dressed in camo."

"That's just awful shit," Bernie heckled. To my dismay, Greenie and Urrie both nodded in agreement.

"You want poetry," I tried again—

> *"Eye witnesses never remember events the same way twice.*
> *So what is truth?*
> *The discards. The misplaced. The words held tight. The cases not solved.*
> *The deductions. Inductions.*
> *Reductions.*
> *The drunk tightrope walker who fucks up daily*
> *The sanitation worker carrying hefty bags full of regrets*
> *The detective who testifies not ready to face judgment yet*
> *Who begs the bench to stall the verdict*
> *To not convict, evict, predict*
> *or let technicalities rule the day."*

I ended, panting. Yeah, this one sucked too, but it's the best I got in me. Still, I figured I sold enough of my sins this week that I rated a freebie. I held my breath as Bernie considered, hoping this poem would be enough. That I should be enough.

"Not a lot of truth in that," he said. "Not a lot of you in that."

"I'm a detective. I live in a world of putting together small clues to find the big picture."

Bernie nodded.

"You a detective or a dick, Sol?"

What did he want from me?

"Both," I said. "Dick," I admitted.

"Hmph," Bernie said. He walked up to the stage, blocked out the light. Beneath us, the boards bowed. I wondered how much sin this demon carried on his shoulders.

"Good enough for me," he said after a long think. "Next."

I was escorted off the stage and not to a chute. My card-playing pals followed behind. Two fiery mahogs led us down a corridor, pausing as we reached the incinerator. Sweat slicked me as one of them fingered the lever. Behind me, someone whimpered a Hallmark greeting card. I sniffled, suddenly sentimental.

Three hallways later, I found myself in a small room with a young woman squeezed into it. The room was just a bunch of mirrors. Not funhouse ones, but the regular kind. The kind that showed your reflection back to you whether you wanted to see yourself or not. A quick survey indicated no hearts scratched into the glass, no stickers marring the perfect reflection. Besides the woman and the mirrors, the only other object in the room was a hammer. They hadn't provided her a stick of furniture, a poster, not even a toilet. Just her, herself, and a hammer.

The weight of the moment hit me. Yet at the same moment, a breath of relief escaped me. Hart hadn't found her. Hadn't recruited her. After counting to ten, I stepped in. Found that my reflection failed to appear in any of the mirrors.

At my footsteps, she startled. Then, she crawled towards me, an expression of loneliness and gratitude blossoming on her face that failed to fool me because her reflections spat and sneered. I tried to shake the fear that climbed up my spine, that all these years later, she still owned me.

Shawn wore her honey hair in a braid and some clothes that were the height of fashion at the time of her death. The glad rags made her look out of date. Don't get me wrong. She was still hot, but next to Urrie, Shawn lacked vitality. Like looking at a memory through a dusty window pane.

As if recognizing something in me, her lips curved upwards. She tried to say something. All I heard was a ragged voice too used to inarticulate screams. She tried again.

"You," she forced out. I felt the Pit heat of that pronoun. Surprisingly, I liked it. I felt seen.

Emotion washed over me. First, terror-filled flight or fight, then a wave of nostalgia. I took a trembling step forward, towards her. The right side of my body weighed a hundred pounds more than my left. My face felt drooped like one of Salvador Dali's melted clocks.

"Hello, Shawn. You look the same," I said. Her baby blues ate me up like Halloween candy. She still had that face, the same gleaming golden hair, and a body in its prime. As I neared her, her eyes flicked back and forth, she licked her lips, and her arms went up protectively to bar her heart. It was what I wanted and what I feared more than anything in my childhood.

"Are you really here?" Then harsher, "What are you doing here?"

Her voice hit me like a rail gun. I flinched. Struck.

"I need a favor."

She snorted. Laughed. Tilted her head back like she was still queen of a middle school named for some forgotten Confederate general. I told myself things had changed. Big things. Hell, they'd even renamed the school.

"Why would I help you?" she asked. "You're a nobody. A little Jewish shit."

A little Jewish shit who got you killed I nearly blurted, but I stopped myself because her insult sounded rusty. So I took the high road and didn't strike back. Part of me wondered if I was incapable of delivering a verbal strike that could land. During her life, I never had been able to do more than cringe when confronted by Shawn.

And I didn't know if anyone deserved this.

So, I stuck to business.

"You know Ronald Hart?" I asked, hating the stutter in my voice. The way my eyes trailed off.

She stroked a braid.

"What's in it for me?"

"What?"

"You want a favor. I got a nice safe room here. Why should I help?"

This was Shawn being nice. She thought I had power. Figured if I got permission to see her then I held sway with some kind of cheese. Still believed in her self-importance enough to think that Hell would eventually bend for her.

Just like Hart did. Except Hornytown had bent for him.

"I can get you a reprieve. A little shore leave."

It was a bluff. I doubted I'd ever get permission from Bernie. I knew neither Urrie nor Greenie would help engineer an escape. Besides, I could tell Shawn wasn't reformed. From the scowls in the mirrors, she was years away from any kind of good behavior parole.

"No," Shawn said, "you can't."

Still, she held back that line of invective. That string of words that she used to call me back when she made me the enemy in her war to save Christmas. Her reprieve encouraged me. I decided to make my play.

"I can offer you company," I said. "Visitations. Give you someone to talk shit to."

Her chin gave away how much that hit her. A troll in solitary craved bones to nibble on. As carrots go, mine was shriveled and speckled with white spots, but I knew if hungry enough, even catsup and water makes for gourmet eatings.

"Pitch," she said, indicating an open door or an opening to ridicule.

"Hart's making a play. Something big. He wants more than his corner of Hornytown. More than just the people he can buy in Washington. Right now, he's gone underground, pretending he got offed, but it's a dodge. I want to bring him out in the open. I want to get him pissed enough to show his mug."

Shawn paced. Her ceiling reflection laughed. Her floor reflection scowled. The four wall mirrors indicated various degrees of consideration. After a time, when she could tell I was getting anxious, she raised a hand to forestall me. From the doorway, I caught a glimpse of Urrie. The demon stood with arms crossed in a way that highlighted her claws. More frightening, her downwards tilted chin evoked *mama bear*. To make the point that she had my back explicit, she strode into the mirror room to stand behind me.

The gesture strengthened my spine. Gave me the courage to not start babbling though Urrie's presence didn't seem to cow Shawn a bit. I guess after fifteen years in the Pit the sight of a seducer lacks a little oomph.

"You virgin dick," she began, insulting both my sexual status and profession. "You socialist asshole."

My face relaxed. Her shots had failed to penetrate my mental Kevlar. Surprised by my nonplussed reaction, she upped her game.

"You get me killed and come wanting favors? And you're going to offer me the benefit of your exalted presence! You deserve to face yourself. Not me."

I winced. She continued.

"You did this because I never blew you. Like I'd ever do anything with a short, ugly, fat, stupid creep like you."

Surprise flooded me. Shawn's blows fell like a boxer not used to throwing punches. I studied her anew. Was Shawn really that six-story building that you think, as a child, is the biggest thing in the world? Was Shawn really just a small-timer compared to the actual skyscrapers I have faced? What if the worst villain of my childhood was a small timer? The revelation settled something in me. Allowed me to say something I doubted I could.

"I regret it, you know," I told her. "I never put a hit out on you, but you're right. It was my tongue that got the gun pointed your way. Maybe with more time . . . I never meant to take that from you."

She turned red. Almost as red as Urrie.

"You think I give a fuck about your apologies? This is the nice room. You want to know what they do to me when it's time for my daily exercise? Well? Do you? Look at me, Solomon Weiss. I was fine just how I was, and I don't deserve this!"

Over the years, I'd had hit myself with these same words,

shouldering a burden of blame that bordered on self-hatred, but Shawn's reflections knew better. They turned their ire on her. Even so, I imagined weight added to my soul. My actions had prevented her from getting a chance to clean up her sin sheet.

I decided to help her. She needed to see herself to get a chance.

"Shawn, you were not a good person." We both flinched at the power of the word good, "I'm giving you a chance to do good."

My eyes fell to the hammer as she reached for it.

"I used to strike the mirrors, but all I got was more me! I hate me. I hate you more."

With all her strength she swung the hammer at me. Urrie caught her wrist. I hadn't dodged. I hadn't wanted to. I wanted to take the punishment I deserved.

"Enough," the demon said, her smoker's voice lit with fire. "He will pay for his sins. You are here because of yours."

Urrie's declaration galvanized me. I was here because I had a job to do. A job Shawn could still help with. I tried one last time.

"Shawn, I'm on a case to stop a frame-up. You of all people know what that's like. So, you going to help or what?"

She sulked. Asked again what was in it for her. Urrie pointed out that not every deal required quid pro quo. I heard a lesson for me in that. Wondered if that was the reason I hadn't left the case. If that's why I kept going despite all the shit coming my way. Hell, Connors was probably filling out the APB with my name on it right now for assaulting an officer and interference in an official police action. My life as a dick was over. My life as a free man might be too.

I smirked, picturing the Manischewitz stain I put on her civvies. At least I cost her some dry cleaning.

Interestingly, my expression seemed to unnerve her. I tried to take advantage of it. "Let's stop something really bad from happening, Shawn. All I need from you are words. You were always better at words than me."

She shook her head, afraid. "This smells like entrapment, dick. You just want to prove that I haven't changed." She stared at herself in the mirror. "You don't want to help me. You don't even see me. No one ever saw me."

I reached out. She didn't flinch, didn't slug me, didn't move. I stopped before making contact. I didn't have the right to comfort her. I didn't have her permission to touch her.

"We never had any good times, Shawn," I said. "Never ran in the same circles. Maybe after this is done, we will. But I have a feeling that the world needs help and you're the one I came to. What do you say?"

Shawn placed her hand over mine. I smiled, hoping my sap did the trick, then I saw that all the faces in the mirrors wore the same cruel expression. I knew before she landed the kidney blow what was coming. I crumpled. She stood over me, triumphant as always.

"Help you? Help the world? After . . . Get the fuck out."
And so I did.

Leads dead end. Witnesses flake. Nothing new about that. I didn't blame Shawn. She wasn't the first person to say no to me. Hell, I knew I lowballed the offer. I went to her like she was a coke-addled snitch who'd sell their soul for fifty bucks even though the going rate was a grand.

As I exited Shawn's cell, the absence of reflected light from all her mirrors rendered the hallway gloomy. I squinted at Bernie, waiting for the hillock to come into focus. While I oriented, he picked his nails.

"Could have told you," he said like a six-ton know-it-all.

"Wouldn't have listened," I answered.

He gave a mammoth shrug. "Her soul still needs tenderizing. Has millennia to go."

"Before she becomes one of us," Urrie contributed, which earned a slap of rebuke.

The violence of Bernie's blow stunned me. His backhand left Urrie sprawled on the ground. For a moment, she lay flaccid as a popped balloon. Bernie showed no sign of remorse. Instead, he growled, "You know better. That's need to know."

I filed away a new piece of information. Demons rose after serving their time. There were no Hornytown storks involved. Just reformed humans.

I shook my head. Seemed like a crappy deal to me.

"So there is no way out," I whispered to myself, "ever."

"It's not so bad," Greenie whispered. "Most of us volunteer to stay. It's better than . . ."

They cut themself off when Bernie lowered his tusks.

"No more secrets or all of you go back in the Pit."

At the threat, Urrie paled so much that her body temperature dropped from hot tea to gazpacho.

"I . . ." the succubus began, but Bernie shook his head, allowing no excuses.

"Get him out of here."

Urrie shook her head. Tried to argue that we still needed a troll.

I was wowed. She believed in me. Believed in my plan even after my play with Shawn failed to draw the cards we needed. Her faith in me gave me the strength to walk under my own steam. I turned down the hallway and walked briskly towards the glass ladder.

"It's okay," I told my cardplaying pals. "I know what to do."

I really didn't.

16.

"No. No. No. No," Jamal Sinatra said, ending on the double negative. The pot shop owner advanced, planted a boot on the rumps of a couple permanently tangled up in their game of Twister. I smirked like an asshole. He smirked back with an expression that told me he knew I was here to make tsuris for him and he wasn't having it.

Being a dick and not a cop has its perks. I didn't have to listen. I swept the crystal curtain apart and entered.

As the stoned clientele scurried like mice behind the counters of the pot shop, Urrie took center stage. Lucky for my side, there is no mention of 'Thou Shalt Not Enter' in The Ten.

Without a care in the world, we shouted out an order for a round of brownies and sat down. Eyes followed us. Sinatra's pretended at being independent, but the "Hart" slashed onto the wood beneath my palms told the true story. To show I meant business, I scraped some Pit mud off my sole and filled in the engraved lines.

From my peripheral, I saw someone dashing to the back, reaching into their pants pocket. I nodded to my friends in case they missed it.

"You got to get out," Jamal hissed. "Don't you know they put out a number on you."

Like a dick I put my feet up on the table and said, "We're just here for a little nosh. Is it a high number?"

Jamal's eyes fixed on a clump of Pit clay glistening on the tread of my shoe. Then, he brushed my feet off his furniture like a bubbe swatting a disrespectful pup. I shrugged indifference, motioned to the back towards the clerk who surely by now had dialed the cell phone he'd removed from his pocket.

"Since they're on their way we might as well stay. Don't want to be rude, you know."

My voice carried the grist of a thousand years of persecution.

Sinatra shook his head, refusing to play a part in our plan. With a snap, he summoned a server with a tray. Scorched, blackened, undercooked dough was set before us.

"Your order, sir." Jamal's spittle landed on my brownie. "Eat. Pay. Get out."

At this welcome, I pulled my hat over my eyes to show off a brim that was as burnt as the fare and Greenie laughed. Urrie smooshed a brownie with contempt and I remembered she didn't do spoiled.

I guess she didn't do spittle either.

Judging by the way Greenie smooshed their brownie, I guess they agreed. I laughed.

"Do you know what they said they'd do to anyone helping the succubus? Helping you?" Jamal tried.

I didn't, but it didn't take much imagination. We gave Hart a black eye by escaping his justice, showed everyone his control had limits, and now we were hanging out in one of his places like we owned it. It wasn't a Shawn-level verbal assault, but it was an insult shoved straight in his face.

"It's time for Hart to end this," I suggested mildly. "All

we want is for him to hold a press conference apologizing for faking his death . . ." I paused, considered. Then went for it. It was another dick move, but I couldn't resist rubbing it in. "Also, get him to promise to repent and study his Torah. It'd do him some good."

Jamal tried to hold it back, but he sputtered a laugh. I felt relief.

Under my collarbone, my chutzpah provoked a pulse. I pulled my Chai out. To both our surprise, it glowed. Not a glimmer catching the light, but a god damned, CGI-in-your-face-I'm-going-to-fuck-you-up-warrior glow.

In the Chai's light, Urrie appeared practically orange and didn't look like any celebrity I'd ever mooned over. Instead of a sex symbol, I saw a pert nose, long forehead, a square chin, and freckles on her face that giraffed all the way down to her neck. "What," I asked, "does that mean?"

Sinatra snorted with the wisdom of the perpetually stoned.

"Means you got a backer, Wise Guy."

"But . . . ?" I continued fingering the silver metal. "Who? The Devil? God?"

Sinatra inhaled deeply.

"All that Jewish shit. Christian shit. Muslim shit. Hindu shit. It's all shit. A starter's guide on how not to be a total asshole. You don't know shit about the real."

"So, you think . . . But Hart chased the devil aw . . ."

Jamal put both his hands over his face and slowly pulled downwards. When his eyes emerged, they looked sober, hateful.

"They messed with his shtetl, brother," he said. "You don't mess with the Devil's shtetl."

I laughed. Cynicism and jade made up my composition. Not faith. "But . . . I'm a shmuck. A putz. A shmendrick," I protested. "Jamal, for all the years you've known me have I ever been better than a dick? I can't be anyone's chosen."

I didn't feel special. Didn't feel like anyone had been guiding me. Hell, throughout this whole caper I had veered around corners like a car with sabotaged brakes. Still, I clutched the Chai tight as a valve on a submarine.

"Don't diss your benefactor," Jamal answered. Then, in a surprisingly serious tone asked, "You really going to do this?"

"I really am." I paused. "What else can I do?"

"If the tallit don't fit. Quit."

I shook my head.

"Look. I been chased from my home. Run out of Hornytown. My license is probably flushed . . . "

A hand fell onto my shoulder, it felt warm instead of hot. I patted the claws. Under Urrie's clay heart beat a human one.

"Devil's not a mensch," Sinatra warned. "Not a good man. You pick up his banner, do his work, even for all the right reasons, you ain't escaping the Pit."

I stood because it felt like the right thing to do. Searched for something dramatic to say. Found it.

"I knew my ending before I turned the ignition of my Echo."

Jamal's face pressed into a line so straight it shamed a ruler. Slapping the table, he copied Urrie's earlier move and rubbed a brownie into the grooves of a carved heart.

"Oh fucking Hell," Jamal Sinatra said. "Guess we can't smoke a bong and pretend it's all going to get better."

A car screeched to a stop outside the pot shop. Armed big fellas exited. Doors slammed. Jamal and I shared a look. It was too late for us to come to an agreement. Unbidden, a prayer my bubbe once recited sounded in my head.

May it be Your will that You lead me towards peace, direct my steps toward peace and rescue me from the hand of any enemy.

17.

Five Hart boys sporting six-grand suits marched through the front entrance. Three carried AR-15s while the other two slammed diamond-studded brass knuckles into their fists. As the last goon entered, he turned to lock the door.

"Sinatra!" You let this grime muck up your place?

Sinatra walked calmly behind his counter. Began to wipe it with the heart-filled tie-dye shirt he holstered on his shoulder.

Seeing the goons growling, I interjected. "Hornytown's a hell of a place," I drawled, redirecting the thugs anger back onto me. "Here to negotiate?"

"Nothing to negotiate, dick." I stared the speaker down, his scruffy beard did nothing to make his face less punchable. "You are harboring a fugitive wanted by both the Mayor's office and Mortalville. Give her over."

By my side, Urrie stood, a fusion of Sigorney Weaver and Linda Hamilton. Regret pooled. For a moment in the Chai's light, I had thought I'd seen Urrie's true face and I didn't realize how much I wanted to see it again. Her usual fused, amorphous appearance unsettled me.

Deal with that later, I told myself. For now, focus on the plan.

"Duffle!" I cried out, raising my hand like a student ready to receive a dodgeball. My voice barely rose above the chime of chakra crystals, but Greenie manifested my bag, and tossed me my weapon of choice. I pumped it and gritted my teeth.

The pump pressure informed me the soaker was almost out of ammo. We never reloaded after the diner. No chance to. There are surprisingly few kosher groceries in Hornytown.

Sinatra's eyes widened. I doubted he could hear anything over the crystals, but he knew. To my relief, the duchess kept my bluff to himself. For now anyway.

As I waited for Jamal to work through his best play, Hart's eldest, a raw-faced, bone-shaved man with a nose made to order and Botox eyes, shoved his way through. He gave us his best blank-faced stare, his best bad-ass-I'm-in-control strut.

"You," he said, trying to resurrect a disproven lie, "killed my father."

I smirked. I don't think it was all Hornytown gravity this time.

Daddy must have laid into him for letting us get away before. Diverting my gaze from the tough guys, I risked a look at Urrie. With her upraised chin, she stood stern as Joan of Arc. An unseen wind whipped her hair. I blinked back tears.

"Are you still trying sell that drek," she said.

Junior winked at Urrie without the slightest hint of a Hornytown smirk. After twelve years living in Hornytown, he bore the gravity as easily as a native. I flicked my peepers in the direction of my demon friends. No, I thought, not my demon friends—my reshaped human friends, or rather, my golem friends reforged in the Pit.

A piece of the puzzle clicked into place and my Chai kvelled in my bubbe's voice, *Yasher Koaḥ. Well done* and I knew.

I knew why Hart was in hiding. Knew what was going on. Knew what all this mishigas was about. Still, I wanted confirmation, so I smirked, aimed, and shot Junior right between the eyes.

18.

A gob of melted Play Doh slithered down Junior's face. Unlike the demon bully boy who still sported the hole I shot through his jaw, chunks of Junior crumbled off like he was an improperly kilned pot. The kid reacted by scrambling to grab pieces of himself while at the same time pressing and pinching his dough to keep the rest of his face from sliding off.

"Golem," I cried.

"Abomination," Hart's demon bullies roared and to my surprise turned on him. They ramped up their heat, their claws going from orange to red to white 'til brittle ole Junior shattered. I stared at the human thugs, the ones with the AR-15s. All three wore eyes so wide open that their orbs threatened to fall out. Urrie winked at me with the smug expression of someone who just won a bet.

I toed the linoleum floor, marking a line with the dust from Junior's head. Behind his counter, Jamal stood there stone-faced though he did raise a hand to forestall a dust devil from cleaning up the mess. On a hunch, I sidestepped to the right. The shattered pieces of him wobbled in my direction. Revulsion churned whatever was left in my empty stomach. I forced it to stay down.

"What about you three?" I said, raising the muzzle of my super soaker in their direction, "Any of you shmucks the real deal?"

Confusion and fear tore through the goons. Their normal asshole expressions faded. Alongside them, their demonic partners lost the rest of their conviction. A demon condescending to work for a mortal was bad enough. Working for a Pinocchio? Now that was downright embarrassing.

"Should we test it?"

I gave my soaker a hard pump. I felt no pressure at all. Doubted that it contained even a loogie's worth of wine.

The goons backed off, as did the demons. I relaxed my trigger finger. Hoped they hadn't paid attention to the nervous squeeze that proved my soaker dry. Empty and facing a mob that could tear me apart even if I had a full tank, I did the only thing reasonable. I stomped on a crumble of Junior goo then scraped it off with a butter knife.

"Urrie," I said, waving her to me.

Unsure about where this was going, but with animated Snow White-level innocence spread all over her face, Urrie sidestepped my way. I reached out a hand. She took it. It burned a little, but I ignored the pain and pulled her a half step behind me. If we got back to fighting, I hoped we'd reverse positions. But when you're all in and you got no cards, bluff big.

"Storytime, Urrie," I said over my shoulder. "Time to let the world know what you saw in Hart's Keep that day."

Blinking in a way that would overload a lie detector, Urrie nudged against me. My body stirred, but I elbowed her back. I didn't need any seduction shmutz on top of the shit Sinatra's secondhand was doing to my head. Her hesitance to fill in the gaps of the story surprised me, but after I squeezed her hand, she relented.

"I saw," Urrie began.

"Don't you say anything," a thug screamed. "You signed a binding NDA."

This smirk might have had more to do with attitude than gravity.

"Let the shysters figure that out," I said. "Talk."

To my delight, Hart's demons barred the mortal bully-boys with their massive forearms. Apparently, they wanted to hear what Urrie had to say, too. They weren't the only ones. Climbing onto his patched up floating beanbag, Sinatra ordered his staff to fetch him some popcorn.

The succubus hesitated. Her sigh stung like coals on my back. Everyone waited. Well, one bootlicker tried to make a move, but he didn't get past the forearm gate. From my periphery, I saw Jamal toss him a brownie.

"That night," Urrie said. Greenie leaned in as if they too never heard this part. "After I finished with a client and was putting away my oils, I heard a scream. It was a good one and I know my screams so I ran out to see what was the matter. Others did the same. I wasn't sure what to do. In that section of the resort, we weren't sanctioned for high torture. So, I . . . I decided to investigate.

"The screams were coming from a backroom where we kept the loot used to grease palms back in Mortalville. When I reached Hart's, I saw him." She shook and I couldn't tell if the revulsion was real or an act. "Without his orange makeup and fancy suit, he looked awful. *More* awful, I mean."

"Stop right there," one of Hart's thugs said. "Don't go no further."

"I remember seeing the horn," Urrie continued, gripping the door jamb while pressing against me for comfort, "the one he had surgically attached to his skull. That's how I knew it was him."

I nodded. A shiver unsteadied the gun.

"Behind his desk, Ronald Hart lay in pieces. Clearly dead. So subsumed by his sin that there was nothing mortal left of him. As I watched, more and more bits of him kept falling off. He looked . . ."

"Just Like Junior over there," I helped out.

I felt her cheek nod against my neck.

"Never knew a mortal could do that to themselves," she agreed. "It was like he was made of nothing but sin. No organs. No skin. No hair. Not anything human."

"Or maybe only the stuff that makes you human," I countered.

I felt her shrug.

"Belial!" a loyal thug hissed, accusing Urrie of being a worthless devil and ducking under the forearm gate before charging us.

Greenie walloped the guy with a brownie plate. Shards of painted flowers flew across the room, but the thug didn't crumble. Instead, his face mushed up. Flattened like bread dough struck by a rolling pin. Like Junior, his hands flung up and he screamed while his perfectly manicured nails tore grooves in the stuff his face was made of.

"Don't listen to her. She's a temptress. She's lying. What she's saying just isn't true."

I dismissed him. Beneath his suit, he was just goosh.

Just a shmuck with a memory of being human made of sin and malice and greed and sloth and . . . My thoughts trailed off as I conflated the myth of Prometheus and a few Jewish folktales.

"We're the bosses," the shmendrick said, misunderstanding what he had done to himself.

"You can't do this to us."

"This mortal stuff," I cut him off. "The clay we're made from. The clay we return to . . ."

I stopped before Bernie materialized to slap me silly.

Instead of treading on Hornytown's corporate secrets or egging on the goons some more, I started edging along the shop wall 'til I reached the kitchen door. I gave Jamal a quick look, but he was deep in his own head, made no move to stop me. Urrie followed me step for step like we were dancing backwards. We turned the moment the door swung shut, but it was a door on a hinge without a lock. Piles of grass, sugar, flour, and other edibles graced the cabinets.

For a moment, no one pursued us. The goons and demons were too content to argue to pay much attention to us. Part of me wanted to watch, but I didn't trust how it would pan out. At some point, spurred by their sense of duty to Hornytown or Hart, the demons would let Hart's thugs through.

There was only one thing to do.

We ran. This time, straight towards Hart's Keep.

19.

On the way to Hart's Keep, I took a stroll through Memory Lane back to grade school ceramics. An image of us draping wet rags over unfinished pieces came back to me. My art teacher warned us that clay needs moisture until firing. Otherwise, it dries out and crumbles.

Just like Junior's face.

That meant the Pit with its fiery tortures served as a kind of mortal kiln. Without it, our mortal clay remains unfinished. That's what the Unicorn, Junior, and his longest serving henchmen suffered from. Every year, Hornytown's mortal population and their accumulating/mounting sins converted more and more of their soul to clay, but because it was not counterbalanced by that spirit of tikkun olam, the duty we have to make the world better than we found it or the redemptive fire of the Pit to cure them, they had become brittle. Like all of us, the Hornytown mortals were unfinished pottery, but after a time without repair, they became brittle mush.

I decided not to verify this theory with Urrie or Greenie. I possessed too many Hornytown secrets already and the only thing worse than not knowing was imagining how far demons might go to preserve their trademark practices.

"Do we have a plan?" Greenie asked, oddly content.

"No idea," I said, but by now I figured the rumor mill had ground up the events at Sinatra's and served a thick slice of rumor-porn onto a whole bunch of demons' plates. Hopefully, that meant more defections.

After a short marathon, we reached the gates of Hart's Keep. The thing looked impregnable. It wasn't just the wrought iron and heavy locks or the barbed wire glistening with poison that snaked between the bars. Hart, just to add a bit of DC redundancy, had wrapped the whole thing in yellow caution tape.

"Come on, goo boy! Time to play!" I shouted through the bars.

Who needed Shawn? I rolled out all my playground insults. I even considered challenging Hart to be a man and face me like a devil, but wisely settled on the classic, "You farshtunkener dumkopf."

Beyond the gate, Connors and a squad of cops huddled with some security bruisers. Her locket bounced against her collarbone, full of horn dust that speckled her bare skin. She looked like she didn't even feel the welts the particles left each time they struck her skin.

After my third barrage of Shawn-isms, Connors turned. Sometime after the diner, she had ditched the civvies for action-figure attire: baton on hip, taser, pistol, and full body armor. I grinned at her, sure that if I were a demon she'd be seeing a mix of Don Rickles, Rodney Dangerfield, and Triumph. With an exaggerated sigh, she approached the gates.

"You're supposed to be a wise guy, Sol. What the fuck are you doing here?"

"Alfreda," I said, aiming for the personal. "We know how

this will end. Hart's game is falling apart. You don't want to be on his side."

She shook her head. At her hip, her Glock's muzzle salivated. With an aggrieved look, she pressed closer to the bars and whispered. "Hart's got it all figured out. The hostile takeover is going down. Not just Hornytown, but the whole shebang. Join us, Sol."

I studied her eyes, hunting for that cult-obsessed look. Didn't find it. Connors remained clear-eyed. Either she believed what she said or she was playing at a different game. If scoreboard watching, it didn't surprise me she'd pick Hart and the mortal home team over the Hornytown Devils.

Bargaining hadn't worked last time, but she'd been my lieutenant once. We'd been teammates. I asked for time. Beside me, Urrie shook her head and warned that I didn't have her permission to spill any secrets. I sighed.

Clients make everything harder than they need to be.

"Give me two—"

Connors unclipped her handcuffs and slapped them against her palm.

Calling her bluff, I shoved my arms through the gate bars with a go-ahead-and-cuff-me gesture. She considered it. I talked fast, believing no matter how bought she was, Connors was, deep down, still the woman I had once known.

"I figured out some new things on this case, Alfreda." I twisted around sharply enough to avoid seeing Urrie's disappointment. "Most interesting thing is that all these demons here used to be human."

Connors paused. Measured my bullshit with her cop-o-meter. Gave me her *go ahead, continue* nod.

"Yeah," I said. "After enough years in the pit they get all red and horny. The ones who stay in Hornytown . . . It's like community service or something. They're like the drug dealers who speak at school assemblies to tell the kids to stay clean . . ."

From the side, I saw embarrassment and upset from Urrie and Greenie respectively. Connors caught their reactions, too. Considered them as she weighed my words.

"So what," she said. "What does that have to . . ."

Checking on the activity past the gate, I saw that Hart's boys had retreated to the front door. Clearly, their orders were not to let anyone in and they figured Connors and her blue boys could handle us. I put the problem of what I would do about them aside. Demons were sticklers for the rules. As long as I stayed on this side of the gate, things were kosher between us.

"So," I whispered, "Hart figures this is the key to immortality. If he's right and you help him, you're putting him on a throne forever. So it's not humans versus demons, but whether you really want Ronald Hart to be your eternal king."

The thought clenched her teeth. I let the idea simmer and placed a bet that even someone bought and owned by Hart probably couldn't stomach the idea that their children, grandchildren, and everyone down the line would be his. It's one thing to sell your soul, quite another to sell your entire family tree.

"Bull," she said, finally. "You're just making shit up. Trying to get yourself out of this."

I laughed.

"Me? You think I'd go this far." I gestured far and wide. "Take on all of this? Take on the Unicorn? For what? What do I get out of it? What's in it for me?"

That stank of too much truth. I rushed on before I retreated into cynicism.

"Look, the light flashed on for me when I shot Junior with kosher wine," I said. "Shouldn't have done anything more than ruin his suit and piss him off, but it melted him . . . just like a demon."

"Demon."

"But he isn't dead and he ain't a Hornytown red. So either Junior was replaced or he's now something else. This is what I figure. Deep inside, we're all made of clay. Out in Mortalville, it takes a few years for us to turn to dirt after we die. Here in Hornytown, the dirt that's us, the clay, is composed out of all the sin we carry. You know all that gravity shit you're feeling? Well, I figure that's our sin turning to sludge. That's why only parts of you feel the gravity. Staying in Hornytown turns you into a golem. A beast of fire and clay."

The cement sidewalk under our feet softened in disapproval. Wind bit at me, hot and unhappy. I felt the chill of Bernie's shadow reaching for me, but I kept going.

"Hart's been here what ten, even fifteen years? All that time, growing more and more sinful. Becoming more and more clay and less and less human. By now, he's mud enough that wine hurts him more than a bullet. But that's not the damned point. The damned point is that he's clay that hasn't been sculpted, fired, glazed, or redeemed. He's just one big fucking blob of sin."

That was it. I spent myself. I wasn't sure if it would matter. I wasn't sure if she would believe me or if she would care. I couldn't even be sure if I was right, but both of us knew that Hart was a monster, had always been a monster.

"So," Connors said in a tiny, self-doubting voice, "why bother to fake his death? Why spend his resources to go after the succubus? To go after you?"

"Because I saw him in all his crusty glory and he couldn't stand anyone discovering his ugliness," Urrie said as if the realization just hit her. "This wasn't just a takeover ploy. His actions have always been driven by vanity."

That idea sparked Connors, but didn't quite win her over. "And none of that really matters," I hurried to say. "What matters is, are you willing to take a chance that life under Hart will bring about some benign pro-mortal period for mankind?"

Connors dropped her eyes. She fingered the taser, her pistol, all the artifacts of her office. I wondered if a person could unsell their soul. Whether Connors was willing to try.

"Do you know what kind of paperwork . . ." she muttered.

"What happens in Hornytown . . ."

"Mustn't leave Hornytown," she finished and cursed like a champ. Asked for five minutes.

As she turned, she ripped the locket off her chest. It tinked as it struck the ground. A cloud of shaved horn puffed into the air. A stride later, in her brashest officer-of-the-law-voice, she demanded the gates open so she could take me in.

I smirked.

"I can't believe the Wise Guy told on us," Urrie stage whispered.

"Let's see how the hand plays out," Greenie said. "There may be cards we don't see."

I gripped the Chai under my shirt and prayed. Then turned a disapproving frown their way.

"You're still bound by The Sixth," I warned. They jumped as if they hadn't been purposefully talking loud enough for me to hear. "Don't go making plans yet. Not while I'm sinful enough to switch sides."

Oweee-Oweee-Oweee . . .

A siren cut all of us off.

I stumbled back quickly as a Ford Interceptor charged the gates. Harts' goons barely opened the doors before the police cruiser drove through. The sight of Connors' blue steel expression overwhelmed me. For drama's sake, she slammed the brakes as she passed us and spun out.

"Get in," she ordered. "All of you."

I caught her wink even as she announced she was accepting my offer of surrender and taking us all into custody. We piled into the car and Connors peeled out, burning rubber instead of clay.

Speeding down the streets, Connors rounded corners of crimson brick, blurring past the neon tourist attractions, and not letting up 'til we reached the fiery river that borders Hornytown and Maryland.

"Are we really leaving?" Greenie said. The cardplayer probably hadn't been to Mortalville since they were alive. Instead of answering, Connors downshifted, clicked the radio, and growled, "Not close enough" when static hissed back.

In front of us, the river gurgled and boiled. I hoped Connors carried a purse 'cause I was tired of trading away bits of my redemption. But instead of catching the ferry or plowing into the river, she opened the driver-side door and stepped out. After which, she strode towards the back growling, "You better be right." Then she popped the trunk, motioned me to join her, and inside the well I saw the loveliest sight.

Three kegs.

"Kosher?" I asked.

"You know it, bubbeleh."

I popped the cork and gave it a sniff. Salt filled my nose.

"Hot damn," I grinned.

20.

Keg strapped to my back, I screwed in the hoses. The thrum of chicken soup charging in the barrels resonated against my palms.

It felt right.

Connors admitted that the DCPD kept a stash of chicken soup just in case things in Hornytown went to hell. No one spoke of it and even dicks like me were kept in the dark. Its presence broke every treaty made between Mortalville and the Devil. The Kosher version of the soup made by the caring hands of someone's bubbe just carried too much love in it. Having not just a thermos on my hip, but a keg on my back felt a bit like being a soldier armed with chemical weapons. Unexpectedly, my lips shook and then I began to daven, reciting prayers I didn't even think I remembered.

In addition to the political problems of wielding chicken soup, there was a practical problem, but the DCPD Semi-Auto Soaker 500, unlike mine, required no pumping and with greater pressure reduced the chance of clogging. More importantly, the thing held enough soup in it to not only cure the common cold, but ping a demon at more than a hundred feet.

Connors started to check my gear, but I pulled back.

"Not my first raid," I said, though my conscience whispered like a nervous rookie, *Hey, boychik, now that you know demons are human, do you think you can shoot one?*

I shoved the question aside because I honestly didn't know the answer. Instead, I asked Connors if she planned to call in a team to assist, but she shook her head. From the cast of her eyes, I read the fuller answer. If we called this in, the blue boys were more likely to come gunning for us than to march at our side.

Besides, as ridiculous as it sounds, pseudocide isn't technically a crime. Might be crimes that come out of it like not paying taxes, but there's nothing illegal about pretending to be dead. Still, I knew deep in my sodden clay that we needed to stop Hart and we had to move on him now.

Sometimes, you arrest the bombmaker before anything blows up.

To the side, Greenie grabbed Urrie's wrist. After a few whispered words, the succubus cast a glance at me.

"I'm responsible for him. Not his babysitter."

"Can't win the game," Greenie warned the succubus, "if you aren't honest about the cards in your hand."

Urrie's eyes sought the roiling Hornytown sky. She sucked in a tobacco-filled breath, and shook her head. "If I can't kill, Greenie," Urrie said, "at least let me lie to myself."

Greenie tried to say something more, but Urrie broke free of the puppet's grip and stuffed her arms through the DCPD rain poncho Connors had supplied her. Kitted out, Urrie looked as intimidating as a crossing guard. Still, we expected a soakerfight and no one wanted one of our number taken out by friendly fire. So, looking bad ass was not a high priority.

At a signal from Connors, we piled into the Interceptor. Belted, I closed my eyes and mumbled a Kiddush. No harm in spiking the wine . . . errrr soup.

Connors gunned the ignition. I turned to my pals. Before this was over, I wanted to see them. Not the mish-mash of allure and seduction they project. Not a reflection of my own lusts and insecurities. I wanted to know who they had been, what mistakes led them here, who they really were outside the card games and gambles. I started to ask, then halted. Considered my own mask. Decided I didn't need to see their faces to know them.

Lacking the words for an effective catch phrase, I leaned back. Connors revved the Interceptor hard enough that it threatened the air like a lion. Then, burning rubber, we set out.

—

The gates of Hart's Keep opened with the schmaltzy fanfare reserved for conquering Vikings. We had debated on hiding under a blanket or in the trunk and letting Connors secret us into the Keep, but ultimately decided to take our cue from Luke Skywalker. I smirked at the notion of all three of us playing Chewbacca in ill-fitting handcuffs.

A goon opened the door of the Interceptor and with a gallant wave ushered us out. Sandwiched between my pals, I watched as Urrie glared her captors down and Greenie crunched odds. As we started moving, my attention turned to the pike-like posts with their spearhead hearts. I'm sure the designers had Cupid in mind, but the effect felt much more like something Skeletor would set up for a Grayskull wedding.

I hunkered between my pals, hoping their bulk would hide the keg-shaped hunch in my back.

As we approached the door, we faced our first challenge. "Thought you were turning this lot over to the District, Copper?"

"Countermanded," Connors shrugged. "First jurisdiction belongs to the place where the crime occurred."

I had hoped for a double entendre, some bit of clever wordplay that would go over the demon's head, but what she said worked. After some deliberation, three bulky demons broke off to accompany us. I told the cops remaining outside to "repent and study their Torah." That appeared to confuse them and I smirked at their reaction to such good advice.

Only a few strides later, my feet landed on the lush red carpeting that led to the Keep's revolving doors. Of course, Hart would mark the entrance of his mayoral mansion by making his guests walk in a circle.

We paired off. One prisoner and one guard. I noted the faux torches braced on the glass, the flicker of cursive in a stylized heart over the door, the gargoyles with their animatronic eyes tracking our movements. By a hair, the degree of kitch Hart installed eased my dread.

Impatient, a goon shoved me. I turned so that the blow hit my shoulder and not my keg. Inside, a twenty-foot-long mural of an adult deer slurping up the entrails of the damned confronted us. My breath shuddered. Hart's Keep was a place good little boys don't go. Still, I walked briskly forward, not risking another shove.

"Eager, huh?" My guard laughed with the menace of someone practiced at tying damsels to railroad tracks.

Fire erupted from either side of us, a showman's blaze that screamed, *Welcome to Hell. All major credit cards accepted.*

I raised both my cuffed hands to shield my face. After the eruption, the flames dissolved into a twinkling red and orange simulation of cartoon fire. Like a tourist, nervous laughter escaped me. My guard rolled his eyes.

At the entrance of Hart's Keep, instead of a reception desk, I saw gift shops. Trendy, expensive ones meant to bankrupt a rich man. Tourists clamored for the rolls of gold leaf toilet paper and sniffed at aphrodisiacs passed around by impish salesmen, but the big seller was the tiara with faux devil horns studded with Swarovski crystals. More of those left the shop than mouse ears at Disneyland.

The goons steered us past the attractions and straight towards the ping, tink, and clatter of slot machines. Step by step, we headed towards the casino proper where players sat at roulette and blackjack tables. Even from the distance of a hundred yards, I could feel the gloom of hunched-over figures scribbling promissory notes while trying to guzzle down enough complimentary drinks to offset their losses.

"You want a go, dick?" my escort said. "I got a quarter for you if you want to challenge a one-armed bandit."

I shook my head. "Don't like my chances," I grumbled. "Turns out today isn't my lucky day."

To my left, temptation washed over Connors' face. The wealth dropping into trays, the cry of WINNER, the glitz, all of it enticed her. She kept looking back, imagining glory and a payday. She was giving up a lot today. I wondered about the odds of her pulling a double cross.

"What's so funny?" the demon assigned to me demanded.

My smirk tilted even more. "I was thinking it probably won't matter. It's going to play out the same."

A world-weary nod. A heavy sigh. "Mortals always feel the wheel of fate after it's too late."

The wise guy in me couldn't help himself.

"Funny thing about fate," I said. "Everyone always misinterprets prophesies. So it doesn't matter what we think. The circle still turns in its own orbit."

The goon grunted thoughtfully then shoved me past a garish velvet-wallpapered hallway where we found a singular elevator. Urrie nodded familiarity, mouthed the words *executive offices*.

"Let me guess," I said, "six hundred and sixty-six floors."

"Thirteen," Urrie said.

"Huh," I said. "Hart's small time."

Ding.

I stumbled past a set of gold metallic doors and into the marble-lined chamber of the elevator. It was resplendent: ivory banisters, mother-of-pearl buttons, and a pewter candelabra set at eye-level.

"Freaking anti-menorah," I muttered as a flame extinguished each time the car descended a level.

After we dropped three floors, a curtain opened to reveal a small brass band. They started with a fanfare before the tenor saxophonist asked, "Anything you gents want in particular?"

"When the Saints . . ." I began, trying to be a wise guy, but

the clarinetist rolled his eyes and I realized it had to be the song everyone asked for. "Fine then," I grinned, "How about *Live and Let Die*?"

They began.

At the first chorus, I slipped my cuffs, pulled a water balloon and kneecapped the guard assigned to me. I heard a squish of outrage as clay slopped out the other side. Beside me, Connors wasted no time and blasted the other guards with a squirt gun. The backsplash fell harmlessly against Urrie's poncho.

"What the . . . " the slide trombonist said and lost his tip by not finishing the song.

Crack.

With a heave, Urrie snapped the chains of her bracelets and with the perfect aim of a succubus, kneed a mortal Hart goon in the groin. Beside her, Greenie took care of the last guard. Their efficiency frightened me. Staring down at the unconscious bodies, I felt a sudden stab of relief that I had never tried to run out on a poker debt.

"Which floor? Are we on camera?" I asked Urrie.

"I worked here, but not for security. The mayor's offices are on 13. Penthouse . . . Dungeon," she corrected herself, "but what I saw was on eleven."

I nodded. Took a guess. Hit eleven.

"Hart's not going to be in the dungeon. Can't exactly hide in the Mayor's office."

Guards dispatched, Greenie shimmied the wine off their poncho as Urrie drifted back towards the band. She paled at the sight of flying red droplets. I marveled at the efficacy of police-caliber kosher. It wasn't exactly rabbinical grade, but a hell of a lot sweeter than Manischewitz.

A tremble of adrenaline shivered down my back. I couldn't wait 'til the soup was on.

Seven candles lit. Eight. Nine.

"How long before they recover?" I asked, pointing at the guards.

Greenie shrugged, "Depends on mud density, but the hole doesn't go away until they can claim a new sin to patch it up with."

I was getting all the good shit.

"Okay," I said.

The elevator opened at eleven. I trotted out, spun and hurled a pair of balloons at the gilt double doors. As I expected, the gold melted, fusing the elevator shut. Then I whipped my poncho off and pulled the semi-auto soaker off my back. It looked bad-ass, not white plastic with orange stickers like a toy store bought squirter, but black and menacing. I checked its hose, its indicator, and gave it a just-to-be-sure shake to hear the slosh.

Okay, I told myself, *Hand's been dealt. We're all in. Let's go Hart hunting.*

21.

After the opulence of the elevator, the corporate hallway disappointed. Painted off-white with just a trace of gold filigree on the molding, it appeared almost humdrum. So, with no reason to gawk, Urrie sped us towards the first intersection before taking the second left. Behind us, our dirty feet marred the plush fibers of Hart's tarot deck pattern. Always hunting for clues, I memorized the shifting pattern of cups, swords, and rods though none of it made sense to me. I did better at navigating the maze above us where stucco Minotaurs and other labyrinthian figures starved.

Beware all ye who enter these halls of bureaucracy.

"This way," Urrie said, opening the door to a custodial closet. Inside the narrow space, the air smelled of lye and lies. I swung a mop handle out of my way. Along the walls, industrial-strength Mortalville cleaners sat next to a pyramid of pink and white toilet paper. As they passed, Greenie's control rod caught on one roll and the unspooling paper reminded me that I hadn't taken a dump in three days.

Constipation, just another fringe benefit of Hell.

"Through here," Urrie pointed at the door at the other end of the closet, "are the golden halls."

I didn't know what that meant, but her words drew prickles across my neck.

"What's the security like?" I asked, surprised we weren't already engaged in a firefight.

Urrie dabbed at her forehead with a length of paper towel left on a trolley. Sucker came back wet.

"None," she said, "unless they changed things up. About a month ago, Hart threw everyone out. The floor's abandoned. Only ones allowed on eleven are the Mayor's staff, family, his personal prostitutes, and some food service people. No nine-to-fivers."

I took that in. Weighed and measured it twice. I hate good news. I hate easy. Easy's always a mirage.

"And this is where you found Hart?"

Urrie leveled a look at me that said, "I found him in pieces outside this door."

I took several deep breaths from the diaphragm. Flicked at the rough bristles of a whisk broom. It shocked me that we could be this close. This close to the most powerful monster in Hornytown.

"Let's clean up this mess," Connors shrugged. I eyed her, admiring her savvy with catch-phrase-moments.

Urrie took that as a cue and with practiced fingers pushed down on a set of ideographs set into the door. After a snnnkk-kkt, a crrrkkkt, and a whoosh, the latch released and the door opened.

Gold overwhelmed us.

Row after row of yellow fangs with rubies, garnets, and beryls set above them to form bloody gums ran the length of the hallway. Urrie hesitated before stepping onto the floor.

Going full circle, she arm-barred me and with a backwards glance that said *Watch me*, kicked off her shoes.

I held my breath.

As she set her full weight down upon the black surface, the mouth of the hallway steamed. I eeped in an octave I didn't know I could reach. Greenie muffled their bark of laughter with a hand.

"What you're expecting? Cerberus? Dragons? To have your mortal soul swallowed up?"

Kind of, I thought.

Stifling an urge to talk, I gripped the stock of my soaker and stepped out into the hallway. As I did, a noxious wave misted around me. Belatedly, I turned around and kicked off my shoes. Urrie gestured at my socks so I stripped those off, too.

Connors pressed up behind me, dragging her left foot as if it had grown too heavy to lift. Me? My own gravity, my own clay, felt denser than osmium. Neither Greenie nor Urrie acted inconvenienced by the press. A twinge of envy added a twinge more gravity.

Three doorways down, Greenie whisper-asked if I needed another piggyback. I shook my head. Something in me demanded I stand on my own two feet. Ahead, Urrie mouthed, "Almost there." And somehow, I drew one foot up after another.

At the end of the hallway, Urrie pointed to a door that stood out for being made of pyrite. Not sure how I could tell, but surrounded by this much pure gold, maybe the foolish stuff just stood out. Fitting that the mayor might hide behind a curtain of false opulence. I chuckled, thinking Hart's Keep belonged more in Atlantic City than Hornytown.

Before I could knock, Greenie barged past me and knelt on the floor. With card-sharp eyes, they appraised the lock.

"Looks nineteenth century," they said, and placed their hand over the keyhole. A moment later, their fingers vibrated. Then with a splorp, their clay slithered inside the cylinder. For a moment, they allowed their clay to settle, then with a twist and yank, we heard the click of a lock's release.

Blam. Blam.

Forgetting that each of my legs weighed half a ton, I dove through the just opened door towards the sound of gunfire. Connors spun to put her back to the hallway wall, but didn't enter. Not at first anyway.

"Ow!" Greenie said.

Around their tummy, shredded bits of poncho hung. They plucked shot out of their body, annoyed. Inside, a receptionist sat behind her desk with a shotgun steadied on a Parnian spiral desk fitted with planking that looked scavenged from an eighteenth century pirate ship. The gunpowder scorch had just done a number on its resale.

"You have no appointment," the shotgunist told us and fired again.

I climbed to my knees, aimed my soaker at her and suggested she make an exception.

"Aww," she said, studying our group through her customized heart-shaped smart glasses, "You brought mortal help. How cute."

Then, her peepers peeped Urrie and her sneer evened out.

"You," she said. "We've been looking for you."

Urrie blanched, growing just a bit pink.

"And we delivered," I bullshitted. "Time to pay up. Reward better be big."

That line got her to fluff her hair and preen down at me. Slowly, I rose to my feet, dusted my trousers, and made a show of re-aiming my soaker at Urrie.

"Solomon the Wise Guy taking a bribe," she tsked. "I don't think so."

"Ten years ago," I told her, "the price wasn't good enough, but I think I just found my lottery ticket."

I don't think I fooled her, but I also wasn't fooled by her. She wanted us to think she was a mortal. She wasn't. I counted at least two giveaways: First, she recognized Urrie straight away. Second, she flinched the tiniest bit when I aimed the barrel of my soaker in her direction.

Forcing my sneer in the wrong direction, I shmoozed.

"Honey," I said, "after I got run out of Hornytown, I saw captains, politicians, executives all get paid. I saw demons fall in line. Everyone made it but me. All I got for my morals was a crappy one-room office that I owe so much on that I expect to see eviction papers any day. Now, pull out a checkbook or bring out the man I need to talk to."

Her eyes ticked with each lie. As I'd seasoned truth in, she frowned. She knew some of what I said was true, but my rapid speech prevented her from pinpointing which was which. Made her wrestle with indecision. Her finger hovered over the buttons of a 1960s-looking intercom box—

An inch away.

A half-inch away.

A millimeter away from hitting *call*.

Then, she shook her head.

"No, Wise Guy. You don't have an appointment and you never will."

Like a gunslinger at high noon, I raised the muzzle of my DCPD Super Soaker and gave her a gush. Her mouth opened in surprise as a hubcap-sized hole gaped in her chest.

Bubbe!

She was more stunned than hurt, but I knew she was about to freak out. The really powerful always think they're invulnerable, that nothing can ever happen to them. When something does, it shakes their world. To prove I meant business, I flipped the switch on my soaker from spritz to stream and lasered off her arm. Then, not being able to help myself, smirked.

"I think," I deadpanned, "a hole just opened up in your boss' schedule."

22.

We circled the fallen receptionist. Behind her, under the shade of a brick cobra's hood, a wrought-iron door fitted with heavy bolts and captain's wheel handle barred the way. I turned to our insider. The stiffening of her posture proclaimed, *Here lay Hart*. I nodded and advanced, inspected the bubbles and welts that ran along the iron surface like the drips found after a lousy paint job.

"Connors," I hollered. She poked her head in. "Do the honors."

At the opportunity to take down a piece of Hell, she unloaded a gusher of chicken soup. The stuff bored a meter-wide hole through the iron like it was nothing. I staggered backwards, remembering SWAT teams exhausting whole barrels of kosher wine with less effect.

Letting out a bright yippee, Connors lashed out with three more blasts, enlarging the hole 'til it was mensch-sized.

Without waiting, I climbed past the soft putty edges and found myself in a boardroom. Fingering a bead of water, I stepped past one of the kindergarten-sized stools lined up on each side of a block-long conference table. Above, the sprinklers drizzled. I checked for signs of arson though no smoke filled my nose and nothing in sight appeared burnt. A moment later, Urrie and Greenie's footsteps splashed behind me. I started, then remembered they were wearing rainboots under those ponchos. "Hold on," I warned. "Connors has pork rinds."

"Don't need them," Urrie said, testing the surface with a crimson finger. "Either the soup's been diluted or something in here's really not kosher."

I nodded gravely. Gestured at the room in front of us. "This look right?"

"Not the water, but everything else," Urrie answered.

I looked up because too many childhood movies prepped me for some spider-like thing, but nothing lurked above us waiting to pounce. Still, exercising caution, Urrie edged along the bookshelves that lined the walls. All of them were empty except for sodden copies of Hart's autobiography. There must have been two dozen copies of that twenty-year-old piece of drek, all of them facing front like display copies.

No compulsion pressed me to flip open a copy and skim. You couldn't have paid me. Well, I thought looking at my truth-sniffing pals, it'd take a wheelbarrow full of zeros.

At the head of the table stood a heavy leather throne. It towered over the stools like some sort of height-based power play. You know, the one where the boss forces everyone to stare up at him. Behind it was a framed photograph of Hart's punim dressed up to look like a magazine cover.

"That's a twofer, right?" I murmured in disgust. "A First and a Second."

Wheeze. Wheeze. Gasp.

I stopped, hunted for the source of the labored breathing. Step by step, the sound mutated. My heart, acting like someone pulled its lawnmower cord, revved up.

"So you made it."

I recognized the voice. It sounded like the one on all those television commercials and that piece of crap reality TV show of his.

Instinct put my finger on the trigger. The farshtunken shmendrick was here.

I found him.

There.

On the floor.

Puddled by the foot of his throne.

Like a flattened Tootsie Roll.

"Fu-uck!" Urrie said.

I couldn't have agreed more.

Seeing our pity, the Unicorn grabbed a string of himself with his melted mozzarella fingers and tried to pat it back in place. It fell loose with a meaty splat. I forced myself to step forward.

"Shit," I said. "What have you done to yourself? All the king's horses and all the king's men . . ."

He garbled something. Greenie's puppet eyebrows rose above their head. Prudently, I dug into my pocket to retrieve my phone. Clicked off several shots. Took a video, too. Hit transmit.

"Well, looks like we found proof of life. Sort of," I said and showed everyone in the room the 'message sent' notification.

Based on the moisture steaming off his clay, for the first time in his life Hart looked like he didn't relish a bit of extra exposure. I guess he was regretting upgrading the WIFI.

"I'm the King of Hell! I'm the King of Hell," Hart gurgled and ponderously rose to his feet.

Recognizing the moment of escalation, I backed away. From his expression, I knew he was going to take a go at me.

He didn't have to.

Though the pics and video were embarrassing, they were also so weird that they could be played off as a hoax. If Hart wasn't such a shmendrick he would have realized it, but Hart was flaky as a piece of rugelach.

Still, I knew dumb as he was there was always a chance he could wise up, so I egged him on. "Oy vey, my little Hartala," I smirked, "you've looked better."

He took a swing with an arm that stretched like taffy. Urrie caught it. Her grip left finger-deep impressions. Hart did not take this well.

"How dare you touch me. I'll kill you all," Hart threatened unnecessarily.

His next uppercut spaghettied its way to the ceiling and my confidence grew a titch. The billionaire no longer had much body control.

"This can't be what you want," I told Hart. "You aren't coming out of this metamorphosis a butterfly."

"I'm not finished. Not finished," he declared. "I'm a God! Beyond the Devil. Beyond you."

Yeah cartoon supervillains, take notes. Get your voiceover training in Hornytown. Between the smoker's rasp and the weight of sin, Hart had it perfect.

I dodged another swipe. This one spiderwebbed the conference table with cracks. I pocketed my phone. From the corner of my eye, I saw my pals take defensive positions. Hart didn't care that he was outnumbered, didn't care how many we were. As a sign of how far he had left his humanity behind, he just octopussed. I flashed back to the stop motion clay monsters of movies past as I watched multiple fists emerge on his pasta arms.

My rational brain rejected this, but despite my shock, my tongue, being almost as dickish as my opponent, couldn't help itself.

"Thing you don't know," I said, even as instinct moved my finger to the trigger., "is we're all born from dust and end in dust. What that means, what that little bit of truth means, is that we're all just animated bits of mud."

Urrie blocked an overhead strike, and with those articulate eyes suggested I start moving.

I wondered if moving my mouth counted, because I wasn't quite done.

"You were always going to lose," I prodded. "All the Devil had to do is sit back and laugh."

An even clumsier blow knocked over a stool at the opposite end of the room. Feeling safe, I continued to dick around though maybe I took my Shawn-act too far because I felt a yank and was pulled backwards by the squeeze of a clay snake.

Greenie ran to my defense, but their puppet claws, even though Pit-fired, weren't as dense as Hart's clay so I found myself dragged through the room like a rodeo clown tied to a colt. My tongue finally took five when I found myself in the air.

Crash.

The conference room table shattered under me. Out of

control, I misfired a shot of broth causing my cardplaying pals to scramble. As Hart smashed me into the ceiling, I thought maybe I was emulating Shawn too well, but being a Wise Guy is different than being wise.

But I couldn't stop. Hart was rattled now, and I didn't want to just end him, I wanted him to spill like a Perry Mason witness in the last three minutes of the show. "I bet Hornytown hasn't gotten this big an infusion of sin in a millennium. Between your payoffs and tourism efforts, it's been a fucking boom. I'm going to laugh when people learn you've never been anything but a fraud."

I oofed hard against the floor. Between his strength and my gravity, the world started to spin.

As if on cue, the fakakta sprinklers increased in intensity. Hart took advantage of it. Slipping, sliding, and cursing, he launched me towards a shard of table.

This, I thought, I don't need.

Then just before I hit, I felt a welcome blast of broth. It melted both the snake around my ankle and the shard. Freed, I scurried away even as Hart's tentacle stump flopped around in the hopes of tenderizing me some more.

Dizzy, I sought refuge under the remains of the coffee table. It was raining so hard that I could barely see. I glared at the damn sprinklers. Why did they have to make things so difficult. Why did they even need to . . . ?

I aha-ed.

My head spun in Urrie's direction but before I could even point, she nodded like the femme fatale she was and with a heroic leap, launched herself towards the ceiling.

Hart tried to stop her, hurling a fisted-tentacle in her direction, but she dodged it easily and landed on a bookshelf. Shelf by shelf, she clambered upwards. I felt proud as a papa when I saw her pierce the ceiling and with a *cruuunnk* squeeze the water pipes.

Almost instantly, the rain fizzled. Stopped.

Cutting off the rain shook the room like a kill shot. At the very least, it was the kind of blow that subdued a perp and got them to raise their hands. Made them beg to be taken to a hospital. Except . . . Hart didn't give up.

Hart panicked. Glooped upwards like a plant deathly afraid of an impending drought. Like a bluffer who's been raised and called. He tried to untwist the pipes, but his gloopy hands failed to do anything but crimp them further.

Frustrated, angry, verklempt, he struck out with the surgically-attached horn once attached to his head.

Dumbstruck and not quick enough, I watched the point come at me. As always, Urrie took the blow. I gasped as one end pierced her gut and broke through to the other side. The momentum pushed her backwards.

The sight of her injury rocked me. Dried out all the dickishness on my tongue. Angry, I drew out my Chai. The little schmata filled the room with light bright enough to make Hart balk. I stood up.

"You're clay as much as anyone in the Pit,"—*It was time to stop fighting. It was time to be serious*—"except you've never done any penance. Worse than that, you never studied your damned Torah. Never took advantage of all your opportunities to transform yourself into a mensch."

I felt a bounce in my step. My luminescence grew brighter. Apparently, it enjoyed a little righteous anger.

"She's innocent," I said, pointing at Urrie. "You had no right to do this to her. To put her eternal life at risk."

Hart waggled all eight of his octopus arms up.

"I'm the Mayor of Hornytown," Hart burbled. "Half of Congress is in my pocket. I'm about to become more than the Devil. More than God. You can't touch me."

Derision leaked out of me.

"And you're fucking hiding because you couldn't stand anyone seeing you how ugly you've become." I paused a beat and I heard my bubbe wag her finger through the Chai. "And let me tell you something, boychik, you're not ugly because of the clay."

Hart hurled pieces of glass at me. Somehow, Urrie rose to my defense again. The shards sank into her body. I winced as they embedded. Then, to my surprise, they melted, absorbed as new clay. Patched her up as if Hart had just given her a sin . . . one that could now never be redeemed.

My phone dinged and I checked the screen.

"Huh, cable news," I said. "Think I should take their offer or should we hang on for network news?"

Hart threw an uppercut at me that Connors pushed back with a spritz of chicken soup, causing his arm to noodle.

"You're a nobody," Hart spat. "You aren't rich enough to matter. Nothing you do will ever matter."

I took it. After all, he was probably right. Still, with a Chai in one hand and a super soaker in the other, the catchphrase finally came.

"I'm no fucker," I protested and drew a bead on him. "I'm a dick."

Catching Connors' eye, we both smirked. Then we crossed the streams.

23.

Turns out the case was about vanity. Thomas Aquinas put that one atop his list of sins. Connors and I didn't melt Hart all the way down. Frankly, I'm not sure if clay can be created or destroyed. Who knows how the laws of physics intertwine with the metaphysical, but I emptied my keg in a bout of overzealousness and so did she. By the time we finished, Greenie and Urrie stood trembling on top of the stools above a salt lake just begging for matzoh balls. Then, with evidentiary care, Connors scooped up an action figure-sized Hart into an evidence baggie.

The little Ziploc rocked as the billionaire shook his fist at us from inside. He cursed a blue streak that even taught me a couple new terms.

Departing the scene, I carried Urrie and Greenie out of the wine-sloshed conference room. Fair's fair. Afterwards, we calmly returned back to the custodial closet, where Connors and I got buckets and mops to clean up. We were worried the floor might have been clay and didn't want all of Hart's Keep collapsing around us. A little elbow grease did the trick, but just in case, Connors tossed a bag's worth of pork rinds on the floor to unkosher the slop.

At the elevator, the brass band played something jaunty from Judy Garland's *Wizard of Oz*. Candles lit as we rose.

As for me, everything hurt.

My pals fared better. They may have gotten splashed a bit,

but they also absorbed a heap of Grade A sin. Urrie looked sexy with the extra weight. What can I say? Sometimes, I like my demons thick.

Outside the elevator, a news crew ambushed us. ABC7, if you care. I let Connors take the lead because I figured I'd want her in my corner later. She glowed as she confirmed the video confession and explained how the sting had been months in the planning. She also let 'slip' some details about payoffs and fraud that was probably going to piss off some DA and bought-off judges later, but we didn't care about watering down the case or the wine.

No Hart goons stuck around to make trouble. They all melted into the background except for a few who stuck around to join the party. Outside the Keep, Hornytown's air smelled cleaner; that is, it smelled more of sulfur than tobacco. (Inside, it probably still smelled like Grandma's house at Passover.)

When we reached the Ford Interceptor, Connors locked up the evidence baggie containing Hart in the glove box, but before returning to Chevy Chase, she offered us a ride to Sinatra's where the four of us got a picture on the wall that we signed with a silver Sharpie.

Of course, there was bad news, too. Bernie confirmed I knew too much to ever leave Hornytown again. Hearing that was like getting a faceful of Manischewitz. I mean, card games are fine, but even a dick needs to feel productive and I just didn't know what living as an ex-pat mortal in Hell would be like.

As I sulked, Marge manifested with something that looked like a contract. Turned out it was a deed.

They had worked it out behind my back. My pals were offering me a piece of Hell to call my own.

"Sol, honey," Marge pitched, "as long as Hornytown and Mortalville mix, we're going to need someone who knows the game. C'mon, bluebell, what do you say? Be our resident dick."

While I dithered and the hairs on the back of my neck cha-chaed, the idea of never having to pay rent again grew on me. I told him I'd think it over, but threatened to run for it if they ever offered me a tin star.

It was a cardplayer's bluff, but Marge looked crestfallen at my lack of enthusiasm. So did Greenie. I guess they expected cartwheels. Feeling charitable and unable to bear making a puppet sad, I let them know that even if I was unsure of my hand I was willing to stay in the game and draw some new cards.

"I couldn't do it alone. I'm going to need some office help. Hornytown's a big beat, Urrie, Greenie . . . Marge?"

"And give up showbiz?" the half-cambian pouted when I turned my smirk on him, but I figured this was always the plan. My new shingle would give him a chance to make his accountancy dreams come true. Later, when everyone left, I stared moony-eyed at Urrie. After all, the case was over and these things are supposed to end with a kiss. She looked a bit like the woman I saw in the light of the Chai, but also like Marilyn and Hallie and Mrs. D with her sexy coach's whistle around her neck, and a host of others. For a moment, I wondered about the person she had been before her death and then about the person she grew into after her refiring. Decided it didn't matter.

As she approached, I thought, She's clay. I'm clay. We're a

composite shaped by fire and experience. Who's to say a demon and a schlub can't find something real? Then, I made a move on her and she slapped me hard enough to knock a tooth out.

I landed on my butt, confused.

"Sol," she said, putting me straight, "I saw the weight of your soul and boychik, you can't afford me."

Then, she leaned her forehead against mine in a gesture of friendship and winked.

It was hot as Hell.

A Wise-Guy's Guide to some Jewish and Yiddish Words

Boychik isn't a chick. It's a boy.

Bubbe? Don't you talk about my bubbe. She's an angel. She's also my grandmother.

Bupkes is what I have after I pay all my bills. It's nothing. I got nothing.

My girlfriend once told me that **chai** is life. For the longest time I thought she knew Hebrew. Turns out she was talking about tea. But like always, she was right. **Chai** is life.

Chutzpah? You got some nerve to ask me if I know what chutzpah means. It's courage or daring. It's the ability to go for it even when you don't know if you have the right to. Good to keep in mind that it comes in positive and negative flavors.

Drek is the shit. Okay, it's more like inferior crap.

You know what **Dumkopf** means. Just sound it out.

The reason we don't use chicken soup all the time? The **Fakakta** matzah balls jam up the tubes in the super soaker. That's right, the silly things just cause problems.

That stinker! That dirty **Farshtunkener**. Keep in mind, sometimes the stink ain't the kind you smell.

Glitch. If you don't know what a glitch is there's been a glitch in your education. You didn't realize it's Yiddish? Neither did I.

A **kvetch** is a putz that likes to yoiker. Fine. Fine. A kvetch is a grouch that likes to pester or complain.

Can you believe how greedy some people are? They want the whole **Megillah**. The whole thing. Me, I'll settle for a taste.

A **mensch** ain't a dick. Well, not most of the time. They're a generous, kind person who goes above and beyond. Someone who tries their best to do more good than bad.

When everything's gone bonkers, gone **Meshuganah** it's probably a day ending in "y."

If you do a **Mitzvah**, don't demand a quid pro quo. Do a good deed for its own sake is how you tell the difference between a mensch and a dick.

After all this defining I could use a drink and a **nosh**. Got anything to nibble on?

Oy vey! There are still more words to explain? Am I getting paid for this? Seriously though, every culture has its own version of "Oy!" or "Ay!" it's an expression of alarm or anxiety.

Oy gevalt! Yikes! All this Yiddish is getting out of hand. I must have been meshuganah when I agreed to take this on!

Pisher A goy is a pisser. A Jew is a pisher. Fine. Fine. A goy can be a pisher, too.

Punim. Face it, a punim is your face.

Putz. A low-level jerk or a shmuck.

Schlimazel. That's me. I'm an unlucky guy.

You know those jeans with the holes in them and the unremovable stains? The ones you love so much. In your mother's eyes, it's a **shmata**, a rag.

Shin angela is what my bubbe called me even when I was a little devil. No, it doesn't mean shining angel. After all, Bubbe was no fool. This term of affection translates as "my beautiful boy."

Shlump. Me. I'm a shlump. A loser with bad posture who's made a bunch of mistakes and is a little lost as to how to move forward.

Shmendrik. Kind of the opposite of a mensch. A Shmendrik is a jerk, a loser, and usually someone who thinks they are way smarter than they actually are.

Don't try to **shmooze** me, boychik. My mind's too tough to fall for that kind of sweet talking. Try using the Force, you'll have better luck.

Shmuck?! Watch who you're calling that! Even though a **shmuck** is a dick not all dicks are shmucks.

They say your **Shtetl** is where your heart is. That's drek. It's just a place, a little town. Home is where your family is . . . even if that winds up being in Hornytown.

Shyster. A cheat. A swindler. In its most literal usage, a lawyer.

A dick figures out where you been and what you been up to just by studying the **shmutz**, the dirt, on your shirt or shoes.

Translating's clearly not my thing. It's not my **shtick**.

Matchmaker! Matchmaker! Tell me a story. Spin me a **spiel**.

I got **Tsuris** for days. I got problems enough to fill a blues album.

Tuches. Don't be an ass, a derriere, a real butt, you know what tuches means.

You're still reading? I'm all choked up, **verklempt** if you will.

I'm done with this glossary? **Yasher Koah**, me. Well done, Sol.

Acknowledgments

The road to Hell is paved with good beta readers so having learned nothing from the tale of Orpheus I want to take a moment to look back.

This novella started with an act of chutzpah. After I finished the first draft, I offered it to my book club. This despite the fact that over half of them claimed that they hated speculative fiction. I don't know if I would've ever believed in *Hornytown Chutzpah* to the same degree if Ed Feinberg, one of the aforementioned haters hadn't said, "I began reading this thinking who could this possibly be for and then by the end realized it was written for me."

As you wander through this novella, you will notice some fantastic litter. Much of it comes from the many great writers who strolled through Hornytown before you. Their insight, support, and scraps of brilliant criticism helped to forge this clay. My enduring thanks to Phil Margolies, Phoebie Low, A.D. Sui, Chris Rose, Karen Osborne, Erik Grove, Connie Covington, Karlo Yeager Rodríguez, Robin Duncan, John Appel, Jo Miles, Julio Urdaneta, VH Chen, Doug Dluzen, Emily Wood, Geoffrey Hill, Joyce Chng, Jo Metcalf, Lawrence Miller, and everyone else who spent time with me in this most unexpected suburb of Washington, D.C.

And no, I didn't forget her. To Alicia. My sister, my friend, my erstwhile co-director and the voice of Urrie, Greenie, and so many others. Working with you has been my greatest joy . . . despite the cha chas, Chantilly Lace, and occasional kerfuffles. Your talent, your ability to listen and to teach has made this audio book what it is.

To Atthis Arts and Emily Bell, I have enjoyed our online chats and the delicacy of your editing touch. Despite a fermentation period beset by personal and professional trials, this collaboration has produced a wine I am proud to share with all my friends.

Finally, I owe a big hug to all those enduring their personal hell. For many reasons, these last few years have been very difficult for so many. That you are here to laugh with me means the world. Please remember that laughter is not only the best medicine but the best infectious disease. I hope this story offers you a bowl of comfort and a spritz of joy.

www.ingramcontent.com/pod-product-compliance
Lightning Source LLC
LaVergne TN
LVHW040149080526
838202LV00042B/3087